Blinded

A Novel

b y

KaShamba Williams

Compilation and Introduction copyright © 2003 by
Triple Crown Publications
2959 Stelzer Rd., Suite C
Columbus, Ohio 43219
www.TripleCrownPublications.com

Library of Congress Control Number: 2003115249
ISBN# 0-9702472-7-3
Cover Design/Graphics: www.MarionDesigns.com
Editor: Leah Whitney & Clifford Benton (Audacity)
Consulting: Shannon Holmes & Vickie M. Stringer

First Trade Paperback Edition Printing December 2003

Printed in the United States of America.

Dedication

This book is dedicated to:My precious angel watching over me Lil' Bobby, my first-born child. May your spirit remain alive in our presence. You can rest now; Mommy is on the right track. RIP Son. Know one will ever no the undying pain I have from losing you. I will always love you.

To my beautiful daughters, Mya and Mecca and my handsome son Mehki, you are the reason I stay on the grind. So you will never have to go through my struggle!

Every Queen has an undeniable loving King holding her down... where would I be without you Lamotte.

To my mother Shelley, to hell and back we've been but through it all, I love you with all my heart and will always be your **"Black Princess"**.

To my brother Kenyatta, there is a time and a season for us all. Yours is near, trust and believe it!

Mom-Mom Lena, Aunt Alice (RIP), Pop-Pop Sunny, Grandmom Porcia, Angie, Kenny Granddad George, Mom Nit (RIP), Aunt Charlotte (RIP), Aunt Delores (RIP), Cousin Tanya (RIP), and John "Pete" King. To my innocent little cousin M.J. (RIP). To name sake Kashamba Busby, only God will pull you through! Lamotte Williams, Sr. (RIP Snotty) Grandmom Florine (RIP), who kept me laughing. To all my nieces and nephews, Aunt Rae loves you! To my cousin Rufina Haskins-Hopkins (RIP)

What a woman for this world to lose but for the spirit world to gain. To Deno Moss (RIP). You had a genuine spirit. I still can't believe you're gone. Thank you for your support while on earth. The literary world has lost an outstanding Artist. May God continue to strengthen your wife Marcie, child and Angie.

To the Princess of Hip-Hop Fiction, Miss Nikki Turner, the original. Thank you for believing in me and receiving my work as if it was your own. You held me down and I will never forget that. I have mad love for you. Know that you are an original Black Pearl and there are only a selected few ☺. Last but not least, to all the young women who passed away in the struggle trying to advance.

Acknowledgments

First, I thank God for delivering me from evil. Thank you God for saving me and using my life as a living example.

Wow, I have so many people to acknowledge. Vickie Stringer, Shannon Holmes, thank you for the publication deal! Triple Crown is knocking doors down. We're about to blow baby in a major way!! Just know that, "I'm getting down for my crown!"

Thank you to all of the supporters who purchased the first version of *"If Only Eyes Knew"* now known as *"Blinded"*. I have a special gift for all those with the original copies. Get in contact with me, www.precioustymesentertainment.com.

Lamotte Williams, my Husband, Consultant, Manager, Publicist and best friend. No one can ever take your place! Angie Hairston (Cuz, we did it! I bet Deno is so proud of us.), Mary Hurdle, a sweet yet compassionate woman. Thank you for expertise and encouragement to write. Cynthia that you for stepping in when needed! Kenyatta Johnson (Bro, you're next. You think they ready for "**Goodnight Monkey**." Stay strong black man!), Teali Moore, keep your head up! College is almost over for you! Armelvis Booker, my mentor and true friend, you have truly been an inspiration in my life! I love you dearly. Cynthia Anderson, thank you, you are a blessing in my life. Cousin Kendra, stop playing girl & stay focused, To Shiloh Worship Center, Rev. A.L. Reeves, you are a Godsend! They say be careful what you ask for. Stop gut punching me! Bishop T.D. Jakes, an awesome man of God, you are my spiritual leader on the road. To my father Randy and my stepmother Dee, I've always had genuine love for you. To my brothers, Buddha, Brian, Darren, Lil Randy, Squirt (Stay focused at Lincoln U). To my sisters, Rhonda,

Renee, Chalary and to Theresa and Robin who always accepted me even in doubt. To my crazy mother in law, who took me through the fire and brimstone to be a part of your son's life... Lois Moore. To my extended family, Jasmine, Lamotte III, (even though...), Michael, Ronnie, Timmy, Mira, Kendall, Glen, Ms. Francine, Mrs. Lois, Ronnie, Ayanna, Ms. Almethar (You are such a sweet woman.). Uncle Mike, Carlton, Uncle David (RIP), Lil David, Sonny, Vanessa, Barbara, Keith, Kim, Steven, Aunt Paulette, Uncle Saint, Leslie, Bubbie, Alexis, Malik, Brian, Bonita, Toni, Mrs. Barbara, Mrs. Elaine, Shana, Shay, (Aunt Darlene, RIP), Cabrella, Russell, Donza, Cheryl, Shawnika, Tiffany, Shawn (Keep the faith!), Charmaine, Helen, Mr. Larry (For believing in me and for buying my 1st book!) Donald, Shontai, Makita, Janice, Dawn, Corey, Tracy (Where are you boy?) Prentiss, Richard, Uncle Edward, Kevin, Dee-Dee, Jimae, Kiesha, Terrance, Aunt Lucille (R.I.P.), Demress, Demar, Deshawn, Deartis, Shell, Byron, Melissa Dorsey, Kiana (I have nothing but love for you!). Rev. Isaac Ross & Family, Milford Revival Center, Foster Family, Fawcett Family, Ayers Family, Stovall Family, Stansbury Family, Hairston Family in Chicago, Los Angeles, Wallace Family, Chittum Family, Miller Family, Thomas Family, Redden Family, Lil Will, Leondre Price, (Congrats on Bloody Money!) DE is representing!! Lakita Millner (Change is going to come. If I can change, so can you.) Spoony, Saundra, Melanie, Kitty, Ms. Linda, Larae, Tilla, Tracy, Darcey, Kelly, Parry, Troy, Dawn, Nicole, Sheila, Marie, Donna, Camena, Wymesa, Sia, Yolanda, Chittum, Nee-Nee, Devon, Derrick, Dennis, Simone, Wink, Linda, Tony Hall, Wilbur, Shannon, Jane, Rob Berry, Pooh and Cooter. Sharon, Emmit, Juanita and to all the Williams family. To my folks in Aberdeen, Roslyn, Garry, Debra, Constance Scott, Juanita M. Chandler, Douglas Green, Duvowel Peaker, Pauline Jackson, Darwin Downes, Elouise Walker, Charles Jones (RIP),

James Watkins, Brenda Jones, Tyrone Wiggins, Bobby & the crew at Supreme Cuts. To my W.H.A. people, Sharon, Ella (I take back what I said in 1998, "This is my league!"), Autumn, Theresa, Ayatta, Lois, Rayford, Alphonso, Malcom, Tim, Word, Badger, Vick, Mowbray, Yogi (RIP), Fred, Pat, Donna, Gayle, Sherise Taylor. Al Jay, one of the best barbers in DE, Larry Morris, Pal, Vizable Image Salon, Emma, Barb, Kathy. My NY family, Pearl Reddick, Derrick, "G", Gene (RIP), Michael Ford, Zeek, all my BK Heads! Newark High Class of "89", To Westside (Known for turning jokers out!), Trance Owens (RIP) To Duce-Duce, 22nd Street, (Will it ever change?)...only the people. Kayla Booker (RIP), Kim (RIP), Riverside, Bucket, 2-6 (which is nonexistent now!) To Dwayne (Dapper Dan) & the Southbridge crew, Hilltop, New Castle and to Slower Delaware Dover and Seaford. To everyone who picked up my book and received the message, thank you! To my girl Yo-Yo, Stacia and 4Ever Blessed representing Hartford, CT (My word is my bond!) Mary Morrison for your helpful tips, Omar Tyree for your words of wisdom, Sheila Copeland for your support during the "Tampax Total You Tour" in Philly, Percy Miller (Master P) for your silent motivation, Monster Cody Scott (An all-time classic!) Sister Souljah, Michael Baisden, Karen Q. Miller, Marni Williams, Robert Holt, Kwame Alexander, Sharon Mitchell, Zane, K'wan, Mark Anthony, Al-Tariq Watson (I loved your book.). To all my literary heads! To Delaware State College, Springfield College of Wilmington, special thanks to Dr. Willis, Dr. Stang, Dr. Gilliam-Johnson, Dr. Hanks, Detective Chapman (What more can I say...it's all in the name!), Professor Mayfield (You have too many titles to name with an abundance of knowledge.), Dr. Roland, Dr. Hudson, Krupanski, Professor Bryant, Professor Andre Bryant (I love your spirit!),

Professor Moss, Professor Figueroa, Rieger, Donovan, Professor Miller, Regina, June, Stephanie. Jacqueline, Rochelle and the people at Corporations. The entire S.A.V. Family ☺ Marvin, Flomo, Monique and Brenda. Amazing Grace, No Baggage Book Club, Mary Hurdle, Lillian Hood, Linda Chamberlain, Amanda Morris-May, Monica, Kim Bodie. Thanks to Haneef's, Ninth Street Bookstore, Mejah Books (Emelyn, you are so genuine!), www.theblacklibrary.com, www.precioustymesentertainment.com. Fairfax Newsstand (Books N Things), Raw Sistazs for the hot book review and to all the stores with this book on the shelf. John Williams and Save the Seed Program. Twin Poets, Anthony (a young and gifted illustrator), Crystal Baynard, Terrell Alexander and Delaware's own Next Level Magazine, Picture That Productions, Corry Burris, my poetry producer, Kyle Bannister. Shout out to my literary brothers on lock down, Mike Reynolds, Keith Watson, Devon Garner, Nyerere Bey, Al-Tariq Banks, Marc Briggs. Most of these brothas write in the **"Connect The Dots"** newsletter for Smyrna Prison. Shout out to all the young ladies trying to get their minds right at the New Castle County Detention Center. Also, to all the positive individuals representing for Delaware! If I failed to mention your name, blame it on the mind and not my heart! I'm showing so much love this time around and some of you know, you didn't deserve the shout, just know that I don't hold negative energy near my heart!

Until next time... Precioustymes!

"Remember times are precious, never waste it on negative energy."

One Love, One Spirit,

KaShamba

Chapter One

The Hood I Know

I was always told that the high school years are supposed to be the best years of your life. Well, that's what I'd heard all my teenage years. Maybe I missed something, because I could never seem to mentally comprehend that philosophy. There was never one semester in high school that truly sparked my interest. Many days I had to literally convince myself that going to school would someday be useful. I wasn't even thinking about college...you couldn't begin to convince me to go. Why in the hell would I torture myself with another four years of school? I was not trying to chase the *American Dream.* The only dream I was chasing was my own, and it sure in hell wasn't to have a family with a white picket fence. My expectations of life were so much more than that.

Another four years of school, oh, hell no; I couldn't see that. Truth be told, I was counting down the days to high school graduation. What else should I have wanted for myself when I was the only one in my immediate family to get a high school diploma anyway? That alone was an accomplishment. Breaking the family tradition of getting a high school diploma was reward enough for me, but please don't get it twisted; by no means was I a dumb broad. My grade point average was a 3.7 and had been since freshman year. And in case you're a little slow, that's about an A-minus average. Like many other disadvantaged youth, I successfully completed all of those bullshit seminars: Life Skills, Office Education of America, Scared Straight and Females in Transition. Guidance counselors began plucking my damn nerves in the eleventh grade, trying to get me to apply for academic scholarships, but for what? Even applying would have been a waste of my time. Scholarships were something that I would never have followed up on anyway. My family was so damn poor; we struggled each month to pay the house note just to keep the Sheriff's department from posting foreclosure notices on our front door. After a certain point, I realized that I was only capable of supporting myself, but the way I saw it, if I left this earth I'd be one less burden. Beside that, I was ready to experience a different lifestyle other than the one I was used to in little ol' Delaware. *Could I live gangsta like the Queens of Brooklyn, Los Angeles, Detroit, Houston, and, of course, Hotlanta?* I was uncertain which city was ready for me, first, but I knew that whichever city I chose, I'd be staying for at least three months—or however long I wanted! Since I was grown, I was in control of my fate. I knew that with my initiative, once I put my plan in action it would be on! All I needed was a couple of necessities—clothing and a few ends for gas and food. The other things I would somehow maneuver however I could from anyone game to get played…for real, straight like that!

One thing I did know for sure was that I was nothing, I mean, nothing, like my mother. Her pimp game used to be strong, but ever since that damn crack cocaine hit the scene, her ass got scarce. She'd be gone for days, too! I remember one time when I was about ten, I watched her creeping out the basement door with two luggage bags, chasing behind her young-ass boyfriend. I must admit, though, that in her sharpest day, she was a bad-assed, long, silky, dark-haired redbone with some sexy-ass Tina Turner legs. The pimps admired her from H-town to Chi-town. There wasn't a state she didn't run through that niggas wasn't after her ass. Too bad I didn't get a chance to admire her when she was in that stage of her game. Instead, many of my memories are of her crackhead days.

I was totally opposite her. I was a feisty, deceiving ghetto queen growing up in small Delaware—the first state, but seen by many as a small city in Philadelphia or a rural location in Maryland. But after the increase in cocaine and heroin, it became the infamous hustler's state—a state that you could triple your money in—twice over! You could cop a brick in Manhattan for nineteen and quick-flip it for a quick twenty-five grand on the street. A nigga with a strong team would eliminate the thought of selling it for weight but have his crew break it down to fat nicks to triple the money. If you bought an ounce for six hundred and broke that down, you could make eighteen hundred.

If a joker from D-ware were on top of his hustle, he'd shop around down in the *Dirty South* for some sweet numbers and exclude himself from any up-north drought; I learned the business early from my brother, Yatta.

We grew up on one of Delaware's most deplorable blocks—East Twenty-Second Street. *Deuce-Deuce* is what it was called—where you could become ghetto rich if you were street- smart and possessed common sense. It was a neighborhood engulfed with hustlers, chicks and ghetto riches. Eating didn't come easy, since meals were seldom cooked in households on Deuce-Deuce. Kids were left on their own.

As an underprivileged young black man, Yatta turned to the streets for ghetto love and support. The streets were open to male membership, but when it came to females it was show and prove. If you weren't capable of that you could forget about respect, and respect is all you had in the hood. I earned my rights and ranks in the struggle on Deuce-Deuce through winning a numerous amount of blood-shedding fights, excelling at pimping hustlers and forming the all female gang, *Won Sumth'n Clique*. We were known for boosting clothes and jewelry.

Dwelling deep in the hellish underground, me, Tweet, Mia, Diamond and Le-Le represented the clique to the fullest. We even branded ourselves: We had *Deuce-Deuce-Won-   Sumth'n Clique~What Nigga* engraved inside of a broken heart on our forearms.

The underground world in Delaware, Westside, Hilltop, Market Street, Riverside, Ninth Street, Southbridge, Overbrook Gardens, Simmons Gardens, and, of course, Parkside, saluted my girls, and held their leader, me, up high. The religious community deemed me demonic, and those on the come-up yearned for my downfall. Since being handed down issues of whoredom, deception, thievery and volatile behavior, I had common sense and Delaware street smarts. Despite what others believed of me, I was born to lead, and if following my lead tempted individuals to live a negative lifestyle, then, so be it.

When the day of my graduation arrived, I felt like I had conquered the world. Internally, I couldn't help but wonder if I should've had those feeling all along. I'm not sure and don't care to reflect any more than I have to. Anyway, I proved all of those people wrong who thought that I wouldn't make it. I even overcame an encounter with the superintendent of the school who made it almost impossible for me to *walk*, all because of a petty fight I got into with this chicken head after school two days before graduating.

This trick, Drea, tried to play me by messing with my young boy, Da'Quan. I had used him for the little bit he was worth hustling, but when his family came into some money from an automobile accident lawsuit, she wanted to try her luck with him. One day after school, the dudes from the basketball team were celebrating up in the gym with some hotties for accomplishing the best basketball record of the school's history. Even though it was months after the season, they were still receiving awards from the athletic division.   Everybody stayed afterward to mingle.   I was alone because I had told the girls I was heading back to the hood, but I changed my mind when I saw Drea's bi-sexual, nasty ass posted up in my friend Da'Quan's face.   I couldn't believe my eyes looking through the gymnasium window.   Pushing the doors wide open, I stared directly at both of them. Da'Quan politely moved away from her when he saw me coming toward the bleachers.

"That's right, you better represent!" I said to him hastily.   A few of Drea's little girlfriends rose up from the bleachers like they were going to doing something. "I wish the fuck y'all gay asses would act like you're going to jump me," I yelled out to them.   "I'll call the Won Sumth'n Clique up so fast and they'll be over here to give out straight beat downs!   Hold up, better yet, I'll take every last one of you one by one...ain't none of y'all ready for this!"

Drea stood there acting like she wasn't moved by my words and then blurted out, "Who's this bitch talking to?   I know she ain't jealous 'cause I did her man!"

I couldn't respond quickly enough.   "Oh, no, tack head, if he was my man, you would never, I mean, *n e v e r*, be able to speak to him, not to mention screw him."

She was trying to get cute by this time because we were the center of attention. Calling herself playing me, she said, "What, you mad 'cause Da'Quan likes to eat out?"

I knew I had her on this one. I said, "See, that's where I'm a little confused." I pointed my finger all up in her face and added, "I thought you were the one who liked to eat out." After I said that, I turned my back to her and grabbed Da'Quan to get up out the gym. I sensed that she would follow us, so I prepared myself just in case she tried to jump me from behind. What I didn't expect was a thirty-two-ounce bottle of fruit punch soda to be thrown in my direction. It went all over my cute, gray BeBe short-sleeved shirt and stained my designer Nikki Turner original jeans. Da'Quan didn't have a splotch of soda on him. I was the laughing stock of the event. She had to get it. It wasn't even about Da'Quan; it was the principle of the whole ordeal. The security guard escorted me out of the building when I cursed out those laughing from one bleacher to the next. Luckily, Da'Quan drove his new car, so I didn't have to listen to his dumb ass while riding home in mine.

The next day, I was prepared to beat the brakes off Drea's ass. We had the same lunch period and I knew that when I saw her, I was going to get at her.

Hold up, though, why did she try to play me again! My crew, Tweet, Mia, Diamond and Le-Le from the Won Sumth'n Clique all came to school together, so I knew they had my back. She, on the other hand, had like ten girls posted up with her. When we walked in everybody knew what was about to go down, so they parted ways before the drama started.

As soon as I got within reach, I grabbed her by the back of her head, yanking her body to the floor. I began punching her in the face until my knuckles started to bleed. My crew watched, waiting for the other girls to jump in it, but they knew what was best. They stayed their behinds far from reach. I stomped the mess out of Drea and then threw a lunch table on her. The school had to send her bloody body to the emergency unit of the hospital. That's why they tried to deny me the opportunity to *walk*, because of the severity of her injuries. They had me sitting in the office waiting for the police to arrive. However, the girl's mother never showed, and the superintendent let me go and told me to make graduation day the last time they would ever see me again.

It was like a breath of fresh air when graduation came—the last day of school forever. I got an instant rush when I walked across the stage. That feeling overpowered any ills and beefs I had with the school and its students. For some reason, though, I couldn't help but to lift up my gown and tell those uptight, unrealistic goal-setting teachers and counselors to "Kiss Mona Foster's Ass" before walking to the end of the stage. Parents looked on in amazement while students laughed loudly. Teachers started running from all directions, wondering which of them would be the first to remove me from the ceremony. My family stood there in disbelief with their mouths open. So what they were embarrassed; this was a long time coming. This was a day they would never understand. All the obstacles and tribulations I endured while in high school had finally come to an end. It was a done deal, and Miss Mona was going down in history whether those bastards wanted her to or not.

After the graduation ceremony, my Mom put together a so-called celebration gathering, inviting damn near the whole neighborhood. Most of the people who showed up were her friends. My dad even came over, even though he hadn't been involved in my life since I was five; so I wasn't the least bit impressed that he decided to show. This gathering was right up mom's alley. She loved to entertain, and that, believe me, she did well! It was more like an old reunion of her friends. They gathered together, reminiscing, laughing and sipping on cheap liquor and watered-down beer. They were really having a good time reliving their youth. A few of them could be seen from time to time go into the abandoned basement to smoke their stuff. The sight of them put a bad taste in my mouth. I couldn't stand them fronting, acting like we were one big happy family. We were far from that, more like a dysfunctional family, on the real! So with my lips pouted, I walked into the room where my few friends sat, and notice I said *few*, 'cause my friends came a dime a dozen. It really didn't matter if I only had one. Tweet, Mia, Diamond and Le-Le, they were all right, but sometimes they showed out, and I didn't like that. None of them were cut out to be down with a rebel like me. They were blockheads and just couldn't see past the block. My vision was too big for them. Most of the time they hindered my thinking. The more I realized that, the more I started to distance myself from them. That's why it wouldn't be long before I would phase them out and recruit some real sista soldiers down for my cause. Until then, they would have to do.

I kicked it with them for a minute and then rolled out. I didn't want to stick around anyway; the house hadn't been cleaned in weeks and the furniture was so old that the fabric had faded in color three times over. Grandma still kept the plastic covering on it, though, and needless to say it was hot as hell sitting on plastic-covered furniture in June. There was also a large hole in the living room ceiling from a toilet leak that went without repair for at least a year. We had carpet that was so old from the wear and tear that you could see the wood underneath in some places. I would have taken my friends up to my room, but if I did that, they would have found out that it consisted of a couch and a love seat. In my absence, this was where my mom had entertained her friends at one time.

Though I loved my family dearly, I could not see myself living like this now that I was old enough to get out on my own. Our neighborhood wasn't considered the projects, but it sure was poverty-stricken. Some of the sidewalks were cracked up and gravelly, and others were raised, creating serious tripping hazards. There were huge tree leaves covering most of the neighborhood roofs, causing clogged drains and damaged downspouts. That's why most of the houses had bad ceiling leaks.

City officials didn't give a damn. They never cut the trees back, despite all the written complaints. Our trees were so bad that from the right of the street to the left of the street they combined together. Cars seldom drove down our street, fearing tree branches would snap and damage their windshields, cause dents or scratch up the paint. Me, personally, I never complained, because every day I saw at least twenty people shacked up in the abandoned house on the corner. I was thankful that it wasn't our family.

Grandma owned her home. Well, at least for the months the house note got paid. Looking into her dreary, dark eyes, you could see the hell my mother put her through. She wasn't an old grandma— only fifty-three years of age, but she could have easily passed for a woman of about seventy. The wrinkles in her face sagged like Droopy the Dog and she was skin and bones, but I loved her to death. To escape her worries, she drank a hundred percent proof Ucon Jack daily. Needless to say, she stayed fired up. It was obvious that our family had deep issues—so deep that a trickling pond couldn't catch up to them.

Technically speaking, all of the families living in the hood had issues, but I believe my mom buried ours so deeply that she convinced herself they'd disappear. Being a mother or a provider never agreed with her character. She attempted several times but it never came natural or seemed quite right. You would think that at some point, before it was too late, she would've changed to at least develop some type of relationship with her kids, but that was too hard of a task for her.

One thing I *can* say, though, she was damn sure a protector. Once when I was eleven, she chased a man up and down the streets into an alleyway with an exposed shotgun, busting shots wildly because he said, I was *filling out like a woman.* Another time she beat down one of her female friends for mentioning that she heard a project chick say my brother could eat the *nana* good. She beat her so badly with brass knuckles that they left a permanent scar on her face. And if she had a little gin in her, you'd better stay clear of her path, because if you didn't, you were asking for drama.

Part of me wanted so badly to prove to my mom that life was not about what was going on inside her little box, and that if she just took a peek outside of it, she would not only visualize success but even reach to obtain it. It was past time for me to let her know I was ready for the challenges of the world by my lonesome—responsible enough to care for myself and smart enough not to get caught up by teenage pregnancy...even though I could have been a teen mom since she kept pressuring me to have a baby— just so she could be a young grandmother and not an old one. Oh, how she didn't realize that that thought was so far from my mind!

Graduating from high school was definitely my opportunity to get away and escape my surroundings. I wanted to erase from my mind all of my shortcomings and look toward a bright future. I wanted to escape those spirits of whoredom, thievery, drug abuse and lack of motivation and replace them with positive ones. I knew that if I didn't move quickly, it would only be a matter of time before those negative spirits would consume me.

The stoop was the spot where I did most of my observing and thinking. From here I'd watch the magnificent hood nightlife. My neighbor, Sheila, would sometimes come out to join me. I'll never forget the night she came out on the stoop, mascara running down her swollen face and looking all beat down. She had been in a fight with her man, Sweetback, or, his fists had been in a fight with her face. She had enough of him beating on her and couldn't take it anymore, so I volunteered to call the cops but only after she promised that this time she would make him leave. I told her to remain on the stoop because I knew it would take the police close to four hours to respond. I don't know why she didn't see it coming. Sweetback practically lived up on the second floor of her duplex, forbidding her to share his bed...well, the bed she provided for him. The only time you could find him on the first floor was when Sheila cooked a meal. He beat her ass every time he got mad at one of his other women. She mainly stayed downstairs, trying to avoid getting her ass whooped.

Several times I saw him sneak one of his nasty tricks from Vandever Avenue into Sheila's duplex. Her name was *Tastee*, and it fit, 'cause every man in the neighborhood had gotten a taste of Tastee. Sweetback had Sheila dick-dizzy. It didn't matter if she caught him in the bed with another woman. Her dumb ass still would've taken him back.

As we patiently waited for the police to arrive, we could hear Sweetback cussing her loudly. I told her not to worry, but she didn't listen and began to cry. While she saw this as a bad ending, I saw it as a golden opportunity to rent an apartment. What better time than the present, while she was in a vulnerable state, could I ask her to rent out the second floor to me? From our many talks on the stoop, I learned that Sweetback only gave her $250 a month toward her bills, so I figured if I pushed it up to $290, she couldn't resist. Besides, she was bound to have financial problems without his extra income.

When I confronted her she was slow to respond, but after making that irresistible offer, she gave in.

Pressing my luck, I asked her to include all utilities, with the exception of telephone expenses to which she agreed. My mom always told me that my manip game would catch up with me, but this time it worked in my favor. Even without a legit job, I was sure to come up with at least three hundred dollars a month. My hustle from boosting clothes and jewelry could bring me that much. But since graduation, I didn't have enough time to go out and get merchandise to sell.

I had male friends who would pass off three hundred bucks on any given day. And please believe I could cop that amount in less than an hour. The first thing I did was called my brother, Yatta, and told him that I was moving into my own apartment. He was excited for me but wanted to know how I was going to pay rent and get the place furnished. He was concerned that I was going out to the stores. I had to let him know that there was no need to worry because shit was about to blow for me, from either boosting clothes or getting with a hustler.

One day I sat in front of my grandma's house, watching to see who would drive through. Tweet had a little toy Plymouth Horizon that I would borrow every now and then, so when she rode through, I hollered for her to stop. "*T w e e t*, stop the car!" I yelled out as loudly as I could. Hearing me, Tweet pulled the car over and waited for me to walk towards her.

"Whassup, Mona? What is your sneaky ass up to?"

I wasn't trying to let her know my business, so I shifted the conversation. "No, the question is, what are *you* up to?"

"I'm headed over to the Westside to see my little friend. You wanna ride with me?"

I did a self-assessment of my gear and decided that the white capri pants, black and white, silver-studded BeBe shirt and my black sandal boots was a nice enough outfit to cop me some cash. "Yeah, I'll go over there with you. I'm trying to see Michael today, anyway. I need some loot!"

Chapter 2

On The Rise

A day after I settled into the apartment, my Grandma made the decision to co-sign a car loan for me to get a pearly, gold-colored Honda Accord. It took a while to convince her because she knew I'd just quit my job. However, I informed her of the possibility of me becoming the head associate of the jewelry department in Macy's at the Christiana Mall, but in order for me to take on the job I needed a car. These were all lies! I wasn't trying to work for Macy's. Steal from them, yes, work for them, no. I needed to pursue my victims the correct way... in a nice ride! I kept telling her that personnel constantly called, trying to recruit me for the position. I was pressuring her for a month or so when it finally sank in. I think she changed her mind because I told her that since they were so impressed with my negotiating they wanted to offer me the Sales Manager position instead. It wasn't like she would be the person responsible for the car payments. I tried many times to get a loan solo, but the amount of money made from my old job wasn't enough income. They mandated a co-signer with good credit or more income to take the car off the lot. Foolishly, the dealer allowed my grandmother and me to take the car without leaving a down payment. He didn't even request to see any updated pay stubs. If he had, he would have realized that I was out of a job and my pay stubs were over three weeks old. The only downfall was the seven-hundred-dollar deposit I had to come up with in seven days. It really didn't matter to me, though, as long as I got my ride.

After a minute of brainstorming, I called Michael, a chump-ass drug dealer from the Hilltop area, and I told him I needed fifteen hundred dollars. It was perfect timing, because I had just spent the day with him making him feel like he was my man. Trying to play it off, I didn't hit him up for any money then, but today I was gon' hit his pockets hard. Anytime I needed fast money, he was the one to call.

All I had to do was spend the night with him. He was always trying to get me to sex him but every time he tried, I told him I was on my period. I even let him feel the pad, promising him that when I came off I would call him. If getting the money meant wearing a pad, oh well, then that's what I had to do. What I also did was jerk his little pinky-dinky like he had a gigantic King Cobra. He said I was a man's dream masturbator and I couldn't agree with him more; when I did it, I did it right—so good that he paid me for it. Actually, a couple of niggas paid me for it! For some, jerking wasn't good enough. When I sensed that, I would give them space—flip that shit on them, put them on punishment. I had the best hand job in town. They had to recognize or get left behind. Not many of them were lucky enough to get my *snap-back-come-back*, but if any one of them did, boy was I in trouble. I would have stalkers for days!

When my money was straight, I stayed away from Michael because I didn't even like him. He wasn't my type. In fact, he was ugly as hell but his money stretched long. Shit, at least I was able to pay the down payment on my car plus two month's rent within two days. My next thought was to hit him up again the following week so I could get my furniture. He was good for that, too. My plan was to invite him over to my apartment and when he'd see that I didn't have any furniture, his stupid ass would feel sorry for me. I'd slow wind him with a little mellow music and jerk the babies out his ass. Without a doubt, he would pass off that cash again.

My behaviors came straight from being a firsthand witness to those lazy, good-for- nothing men my mama would bring home. She had the kind of men who stuck around just long enough to hit it, and after a month or so they'd be history; or, she would bring home the type that wanted her to cater just to them. The surprising part is that she did her damn best to please them, even though none of them came out their pockets. She courted men like she cashed her welfare check. And every month she had a new man while still living at home with her mother, escaping the mere responsibility of being a parent and maintaining a household.

Mom stayed with a straw up her nose, along with our fathers, but that's another story. Half the time we forgot they existed. I didn't know much about my father other than people saying that I looked and acted just like him. But what difference did that make to me? If I never spent time with him, how could I know what he was like?

I hated most of the men my mama would bring home. That's another reason why I couldn't wait to get out of my grandma's house. I was tired of seeing those no-good-ass, old run-down pimp look-alikes, always giving me those grimy seductive looks like I was fresh meat to put on the block. On one of many *strange-man* occurrences, a dude named Eddie came to see my mom. I opened the door and stuck my head through what should have been glass in the storm door, but it was missing. "Yeah, what do you want?" I asked him.

"Is your mother home, young lady?" asked the big, fat, ugly pink-lipped man.

"No, she's not here." I then tried to shut the door, but he forced it back open. "What are you doing?" I replied. His strength outdid mine, so I eased off the door. "I told you my mother's not home, so you'll have to come back later when she's here!" I raised my voice out of fear, and luckily, for me, I kept a golf club behind the front door that I stole from a golfer's bag when his car was left unlocked. When Eddie decided that he was going to come in regardless of what I said, I let him take two steps in and *w h o o p*! I busted him dead upside his head with it. Blood gushed all over the door and carpet. How coincidental was it that my mother was coming up the street. When she saw all the commotion she flew down the block.

"What happened?" she screamed hysterically.

"That daughter of yours is crazy as hell! I don't know what the hell her problem is. I was just trying to leave some money for you." Eddie tried to convince my mother and when he mentioned money, I knew she would believe his story.

"Mona, what the hell is wrong with you? Why the hell would you bust the man upside the head like that? He's going to need about thirty or more stitches to close that gash up." She turned to Eddie. "Eddie, don't worry about it, I'm going to get somebody to take you to the hospital. Now, what did you stop by for again?" She was trying her best to get the money before he went off to the hospital.

"I had this for you." He dug into his back pocket while the blood trickled down his arm. He pulled out eight twenty-dollar bills. "Here, this is for you. Now, do you think you can get one of your neighbors to drive me over to the emergency room at the hospital?"

She snatched up the money before he changed his mind. Then she again tried to act like she was concerned about his health. "I'll see what I can do for you, Eddie. Mona, take your little ass to your own apartment...over here starting trouble with people!"

"I don't care!" I screamed. "He had no business trying to bust all up in the house when you weren't home." You need to ask him about that instead of worrying about what kind of money he had for you."

"Who are you getting fresh-mouthed with, little girl?" my mother snapped back.

"I'm not getting fresh-mouthed. I just need for you to understand that money isn't everything...I mean, going against your daughter for some ends. Come on, now, this must be a joke. I can get you a few dollars, 'cause that's all he's worth. I have friends that will give me quadruple that minute amount." I didn't want to disrespect my mother, but those inner feelings started to rise. "How can you sit there and take up for this man you hardly know? I've been your daughter for eighteen years and you can just turn on me like that. I'm your blood. I came from your flesh." Tears started to fill my eyes, but I refused to let her see me break. I couldn't give her the satisfaction of knowing that I needed healing in my heart from all of the occurrences such as this one.

"Mona, cut the bullshit and go on upstairs or outside somewhere." With a stern look on her face she added, "And for the record, baby girl, of course you get more money...you're young, fresh and new. Men like firm skin—free from cellulite and stretch marks. If it hadn't been for you and your brother, I might still have my shape. But you can keep messing with those little boys if you want...you'll mess around and take on the name slut!"

"Like mother like daughter," I responded without thinking. My mother backhanded me so fast that I saw stars, the moon and black dots all throughout the room.

"Hold the hell up! As long as I live, I don't care if I'm two pounds smoking crack in a closet, don't you ever come at me like that in your life, or you will live to regret it. And another thing, like I said, ain't nobody, including you, going to come between me and Mr. Green." She flashed the money he had given her in my face and totally dismissed my feelings. Somewhere down the line, God would somehow change the situation for me. Normal kids didn't live like this—at least that was my thought.

At thirteen I had a summer job, and would you believe my mom made me pay her every week for sleeping in my own room? She called it her *entertainment* room. She used her welfare check to buy drugs and liquor for partying. The food stamps were hardly ever used to buy groceries for the house. Normally, she sold them. The responsibility of buying food was left to my grandmother. Luckily, she was able to bring leftovers from her job, alleviating some of the food expenses. Grandma worked long hours day after day trying to maintain the bills and take care of us. My brother was four years older than me and mainly stayed away, spending the majority of his time with one of his many girlfriends in the Riverside Projects or out hustling till the wee hours of the morning. This was okay, considering our living arrangements at home.

Riverside Projects were always known for providing affordable housing to families with little to no income. They also housed over seventy percent of the drug dealers in Wilmington. Crackheads and hustlers lived for the excitement in Riverside. There was never a dull moment. The projects looked the same as other low-class housing in bigger cities. They had chocolate brown doors and ugly-ass, orange ceramic floor tile throughout the unit. But at least over there, my brother got a chance to sleep in a bedroom. At home the living room floor was primarily his spot. Sometimes we would joke about not having beds, let alone a room to call our own, just to ease our pain. There were times when I was ready to go to bed but couldn't, because Mom had company in the room. Those were the days she would give me the look, like, *your little ass ain't sleeping in here tonight!*

That was cool because I didn't feel like hearing those nasty sex sounds that she made. Sometimes I thought she was fronting, just trying to make her man feel like he was doing the job by always hollering, "Ooh, aah, that's right, Daddy, give it to me. Hit this pussy, beat it up, give it to Rhonda good!" Many nights the downstairs, plastic- covered sofa felt my presence. I would often cry myself to sleep and pray that things would change. Sometimes I visualized myself living with a well-to-do or middle class family. It really didn't matter, as long as they showed me love. I lacked love. I wanted to be hugged and told that I was beautiful by someone other than a man feeding me an illusion. I needed it from my mother and father, but they were never there when I needed them most. I hurt badly, and the hurt feelings made me hurt others in turn. I thought that in time, maybe I'd be able to help young women like myself. I knew I could, I'd proven that. What would be simpler than running a group home for disadvantaged women? Yeah, that was the plan after I finished my running—to open a group home filled with so much love that everybody in the neighborhood would feel it. I'd be the first person in the Foster family to own and operate their own business.

It wasn't that my family wasn't decent; they just allowed the wiles of the hood to take them under. My brother and me were both products of this environment. Being the first person in my immediate family to graduate was one for the Foster history books. I knew that one day I was bound to do great things, like appear in the infamous Precioustymes Entertainment newsletter, *From My Hood To Your Hood* column. Everyone from hoods around the world would read about my success and how I triumphed in their feature story, usually based on people who overcame major obstacles, students that excelled academically, and, of course, Black-on-Black violent crime. Things were slowly progressing, and for the first time since graduation, I felt good about myself.

Chapter 3

Philly, Philly

"Y ou know Controversy is in town tonight, and to celebrate you buying a car and moving into your own apartment, I got us two tickets to the show...so what's up?" Nee said with enthusiasm.

I must have been making too much noise, hollering and jumping around, 'cause Sheila hit the ceiling trying to get me to simmer down. "Come on, Nee, you don't even have to ask me no shit like that. You know I'm down! I need to go to the mall, though, to get something new to wear. Maybe this time we'll get recognized. Well, *I* might get recognized because I come without the excess baggage," I said very arrogantly.

Nee laughed and said, "Girl, you are dumb! I think I'll wear a pair of black jeans and a T-shirt. It's going to be a bunch of wild-ass people acting like they done lost their minds anyway. I want to be comfortable."

"Well you go right ahead and look like a project bitch if you want to. I'm going to get a beige linen outfit and a pair of brown and beige strap up sandals, because beige always looks good on me, plus it brings out my caramel skin tone," I said smiling.

"Whatever! And where, might I ask, are you going to get the money?" Nee said.

"I guess you think I don't have any pull. What's up with that? You know I've always been above the average bitch. Besides, I did have a job three weeks ago, and my brother, Yatta, paid me seven hundred dollars for stashing his pack last night."

"You still into that shit!" she said with an attitude.

"Trick, don't front, you just mad 'cause my brother won't let you hold nothing and you gave up the pussy for free! So whatever you're thinking, I don't give a fuck. You know you can't front on me, 'cause I always get mine from a nigga without giving up the ass unless I want to. Anyway, you just jealous," I said frowning up my face.

Nee's weak ass could never get a decent man. She always had those niggas best for one-night stands.

Even with that, they never had shit going for themselves, just bum-ass niggas. I tried to put her down with a little taste of game but she was a slow learner. I didn't complain much because out of all my friends she was the best one, even though she really was   a sucker for a man. Me, on the other hand, I was reared to have high expectations from any man, young, middle-aged or old. If they wanted to be with me, they had to have steady money.   I didn't care how they got it; they just had to have it.

When we arrived in Philly, the night was clear and the air was fresh and warm. You could feel the excitement from the concert standing outside of the arena. Parked in the V.I.P. area were several BMW's, Benz's and limousines. I was flabbergasted by the fact that I was so close to meeting Controversy. I didn't need alcoholic beverages or weed to wire me up 'cause my adrenaline gave me a natural high.

Nee just stood there in amazement, as this was her first rap concert. I had been to several; however, this was going to be the one that I would never forget. She took my advice on getting a new outfit—at my expense. It was cool, 'cause she was representing me that night. But don't think for one minute that I didn't make a mental note of her borrowing money from me. In the long run she would pay it off. We did have front row seats, though, which meant a perfect view of the concert. I had to give her credit for that.

Several of the guys were standing in the hallways observing the young ladies as they walked by. All you heard was, "Damn, look at that bitch," or "Damn, she phat as a motherfucker!" Any real woman would have given them nasty looks, but most of the girls smiled flirtingly, knowing they were gaining attention.

I knew I looked good. You couldn't tell me anything that night. My hair was freshly cut in a chic style, wrapped smoothly around my cheekbones. My face was lightly made up to accent my apparel and my light brown eyes glistened under the interior lights. I was a size twelve, and a thick size twelve, for real. My hips were shapely and my ass was round and firm. The sandals tightly secured my thick thighs with their long straps. I felt like a freshly wrapped caramel lollipop, waiting to get torn open and sucked on. I even had all of my jewelry cleaned for this event. Looking over at Nee, I had to admit that although she had a daughter, her figure was still very shapely.

When we approached our seats I instantly noticed this cutie. I later found out that his name was Camron. He was standing in the center of some guys. You could tell they had money from their stance, jewels and clothing. He talked with a New York accent that sent chills deep within my body. I didn't know what it was about a New York accent, but it drove me wild.

"Nee, do you see that guy?"

"All these men in here, which guy are you talking about, girl? There you go again, letting your slut mentality take over," she added, turning her head in every direction.

"Be quiet, the one standing right in the middle. He must be the commander or something—the man in control...ooh, girl, I love him already!"

"Girl, you need to control your lust. I thought you came to get with Controversy."

"I did, but you always need a Plan B; see you wouldn't know about that 'cause you're still stuck on Plan L—losers!"

I grabbed her to get her attention. "Look, look, they have backstage passes! There's our ticket to get backstage."

"Mona, he is not paying you any attention."

"Jealousy will get you nowhere," I replied. "Watch this!"

The arena was filling up quickly as people made their way to their seats. I boldly strutted my ass right over to where the guys were positioned. "Excuse me." It was like they were students in a classroom and I was their teacher, because they all turned around and gave me their full attention. "Damn, what a handsome bunch of young men," I thought as I quickly scanned them. My attention quickly gravitated to the center man. Nee stared in admiration as I pursued my victim. "I couldn't help but notice that you have backstage passes. I'm trying to get backstage to meet Controversy. I'd like to talk to him about a business venture I'm hoping he'll invest in."

I was lying my ass off. This was the twenty-two fake-out to get backstage. The center man looked me directly in the eyes, positioned his toothpick, sucked his teeth and slowly licked his lips. "Pardon me, paw, while I take care of shawtee," he said to his friends. They all stepped aside and walked over to the empty seats by Neika. "What's your name, shaw'tee?"

"My name is Mona, and yours?"

"Camron, but they call me *Cam* for short. What kind of business venture?"

"I want to open a group home for disadvantaged girls. I need funding to start it, though. Do you think he would be interested in my plan?" I asked charismatically.

"Seems like you selling yourself short, trying to get backstage to sell an idea to a rapper. You know damn well that's not what kind of help he'll think you're looking for. What you need is a real man, making honest money to help you out—preferably me," he responded.

"What?" I said with a slight frown. "I know this dude isn't trying to clown me," I thought. The dance floor was packed by now and the music was getting loud.

"I love your idea, and the fact that you're young and beautiful doesn't hurt at all...community service...that's love. I think I could get to like you," he said, moving closer to me. "Come closer, I don't bite," he said devilishly.

"Do you have teeth?"

"Huh", he answered, puzzled. "Of course, I have teeth."

"Then you bite." I smiled back at him with the same devilish grin he gave me.

"Good one, ma," he said. "You're smart. I like that."

"Should I be flattered or pass this off as weak game?"

"My game is tight, ma, you'll never figure it out," he responded confidently. "And   Controversy is preoccupied, but his crew is not."

"Good, then you can put me on," I said with assurance.

"I will if you promise me one thing." He grabbed his bulging love muscle as he spoke.

"And what's that?" I replied.

"Stay with me tonight."

"Stay with you tonight...nigga you must be out of your mind. I just met you. I'm not that hard pressed to meet him like that. And, please calm down, baby, I'm not that groupie chick waiting to get sexed." He was so certain that I would submit to his wish judging by the look on his face.

"Well, if you want to meet Controversy, you'll have to stay with me."

"Why?" I responded.

"Luscious, we are his crew," Cam said.

"Luscious?"

"That's a cute little pet name. It suits you well and it sounds cute."

I smiled, knowing that at least I was getting closer to him. "All right, then, I'll tell you what, slide me your information and if I'm interested I'll get at you, but until then, let me enjoy the show," I said. I was impressed, but I couldn't let him see it. There was a time I would have done practically anything to get backstage without faltering. However, I wanted to play my cards carefully with him. He was a heavy prospect.

"Where are you sitting?" he asked.

"Right over there," I said pointing in the direction of his posse. "I'm sitting right in the same area as your friends."

"That's butter. My seat is over there too, boo."

I could feel him admiring my style as I walked in front of him to the seats. The concert was about to begin. While Euro was performing, Camron motioned for us to head backstage. Camron's brother, Kenny, had won Nee over in no time. Honestly, any man giving her attention would have. I made a gesture, giving her the 4-1-1 that we were going backstage, but she seemed to be in deep conversation with Kenny. Before I could gain her attention, Camron waved impatiently for me to come on, so I left well enough alone. It didn't bother me, as long as I was getting backstage. He was showing his lack of temperance, and I never even noticed.

Backstage was so lively. It was better than being in the general audience. The music was blasting and girls and guys were stationed against the wall getting their talk on. I turned to Camron and asked, "When we gon' meet Controversy's crew?" He just smiled.

"I told you before, you *are* with his crew, sweetheart. Controversy is about to perform, so you'll get a chance to meet him before he goes on."

My heart almost stopped. I was finally going to meet this *knucka*. I tried to hold my composure because I didn't want him to see me in a weak state. I couldn't wait to tell Nee the news; not only did I luck up on a cutie, but he was also a member of Controversy's crew.

"Yo, wait till you see all these groupies trying to get us on the strength of this nigga," Cam said. "I hate groupie bitches. They'll fuck and suck the whole crew just for popularity. He doesn't give a fuck about none of those bitches." My excitement died down after Camron made his comment. "That nigga ain't making nearly as much as I am." I could tell he was hating on Controversy for his own personal gain. "I'm that nigga you want to stay down with." Just as Camron opened the door to the suite, I saw Controversy standing beside his deejay drinking a forty-ounce. My mouth dropped open and I couldn't help but stare. I was speechless. Camron broke the silence. "What up, Paw? You ready to do this or what?"

"Hell, yeah, nigga, let's light this motherfucker up," Controversy stated. He had a buzz from smoking and drinking. "What up, shaw'tee?" he said, as he passed me the forty-ounce before turning and walking toward the center stage. I couldn't get one syllable to come out of my mouth. Nee was laughing so hard she started choking.

"I know *miss bad ass* isn't lost for words."

"Shut up!" I said with disappointment as we walked to our seats. At least I got his forty-ounce. Positioning the forty gently to my lips, I licked the rim slowly as if it were Controversy himself. Closing my eyes, I could taste his breath...it was a heavenly moment. No one even noticed. That night I never got a chance to converse with Controversy, but I did gain an unforgettable acquaintance.

When I heard the sound of Controversy testing his microphone before coming onstage, I panicked. Everything Cam said went in one ear and out the other. I wasn't trying to play myself, but I was jumping up, down and around in my seat. I don't think Cam liked it much; every so often I could see him cutting his eyes at me. As soon as Controversy hit the stage I was all his. He was watching me. I knew he was, and I could feel his eyes exploring me. Nee and I danced to the tunes of his new track, letting Cam and Kenny feel all over our butts. On one song, I bent completely over and worked Cam's ass over. He couldn't handle all the ass that was being thrown at him. I stole the show. I know 'cause Controversy was so impressed with my moves that he put the spotlight on Cam and me while I danced in front of him with my magnificent glow. His eyes were glued on me for the rest of the night.

Chapter 4

The Catch

Camron and I became very close friends. You know, the kind that's like your man but without the title. This was the first time I had a boyfriend who was a major figure. I mean, I had plenty of hustler friends, but they weren't making major money like Cam. I fed Cam's ego every day, be it by phone call, giving him constant attention or just plain wild and freaky sex. You name it; I fed it and doctored it so he could make me his woman. I never put anything or anyone before him. I remember the first time he met my mother, boy, was she a sight to be seen. She looked a hot mess...I mean a *hot mess*. Her hair was braided back in four big dukey braids. It looked like she'd just come home from an all nighter at the crack house. I was so embarrassed, and Cam knew it from my facial expression. She was all up in Cam's face, talkin' 'bout, "Oh, you the new nigga screwing my daughter. I figured she had some big shot with all the new stuff I see her bringing into her little apartment. How much did you pay for that platinum chain around your neck, or is that sterling silver? Nowadays you never know. In my time, we wore the real shit, not that generic shit y'all young kids wearin' today. What y'all about to do anyway, go upstairs and get freaky? If you plan on sexing my daughter, you know you have to pay me at least a hundred dollars, right?"

Cam shook his head. Instead of giving her a hundred, he gave her five hundred and told her, "I'm not giving you the money to sex your daughter. I'm giving you the money so you can get what you need. I can tell you need something if you're trying to sell your daughter. That's real cold. Your baby, or babies should never have a price on them." I wanted to cry, but my pride wouldn't let me. Cam wrapped his arms around me and told me I never had to worry about that again. He told me he was going to take me under his wing and no one would ever hurt me again but him. I made him promise that, but I ignored his last comment about him hurting me.

Although he was from Brooklyn, New York, he rented a condo off of City Line Avenue in Philly for almost a year. The neighborhood was definitely occupied by Philly's most elite. It was no surprise when Camron told me of his involvement in the drug-trafficking business. I knew that from the time I set my eyes on him—especially when he told me he wasn't on Controversy's payroll. He just hung out with him to kill some time and to gain clientele worldwide. His power and success in the drug game intrigued me. I never saw him physically involved. He had his soldiers in command take care of sorting, packing and testing. Never once did he sample his product, which is part of the reason why he became so successful at making that money. His business empire had blossomed in less than one year.

There were thirty-five men stationed in Brooklyn, thirty men stationed in Newark, New Jersey, and twenty men stationed in Philly. Every week we met with his lieutenants at various spots to check up on things. I was never uptight or afraid because I loved living on the edge. Besides, I felt like a queen. Camron made sure that my hair was done every week and I stayed jazzy in the latest styles. In my pocketbook, I always carried at least a thousand dollars daily. It wasn't long before I gave up my little apartment and moved in with Camron. Well, he didn't actually ask me to move in. I just slowly transferred my items to his condo. I knew there was more to life than small Tell-aware.

Rumors were going around town that I was dating one of New York's prominent drug lords. My best friend, Nee, wasn't jealous, but she was mad as hell because of all the time I spent with Cam. I put the chicks from the Won Sumth'n Clique to the side and told them to step up their game without me 'cause I had better things to do. My brother, Yatta, was heckling me to stop fucking with Cam 'cause he heard he was a stone killer. I wasn't sure if that was a good move because of all the things he was doing for me. I didn't need Michael, Troy, Do Good, Kevous, Tye, Leonard or anyone of those Delaware hustlers anymore. The money Cam was passing off, none of them could top.

Yatta had a thing against New York niggas ever since they came and took over one of his spots on Market Street. But I kept his comments about Cam on reserve; what he said was not at all exaggerated. During one of his many episodes of playing spades, I witnessed Camron stab a man directly in his jugular vein for cheating, so I wasn't too quick in making any serious commitments to him. I had an idea that it didn't matter if I wanted a commitment or not. I felt like I had already unofficially committed myself to him. The way we smothered each other with attention, neither of us wanted anything different.

Camron's operation was so large. I later introduced him to my brother and the Westside ballers on Fifth the Forklift. They were already making money but were waiting for the chance to move weekly kilos versus moving them on a monthly basis. I warned them about how Camron was and vowed to them that if they ever came up short to be prepared to come up missing. He was serious about his cheddar. My brother had some ill feelings about me putting him on to Fifth Street, but as far as I was concerned, it was more money for them. He was helping Delaware rise on the map. I was tired of our niggas being called petty hustlers.

My Honda advanced to a bronze colored Grand Cherokee. What more could I ask for? My status in Delaware escalated to new levels. I was now considered one of Wilmington's top ten most sought-after females. At that point, I could've had any baller I wanted. Females from other parts of town were jealous and envious. Every time Camron and I came around they put on their best image trying to get his attention. It was pleasing to me because that made me feel more like a queen. It wouldn't have mattered if he *did* holla at any of them, just as long as I wasn't around. And despite all the cats purring, he had much respect for me in Delaware.

When Controversy had concerts Camron and his crew were always present, but I was forbidden to go. He claimed he didn't want to entice me any more than I needed to be. My infatuation for Controversy was still there, but I kept it more reserved while with Cam.

When we weren't cruising around to handle business we would escape to visit his peeps in Jamaica. The first time we flew out of Philadelphia International Airport, he hadn't revealed to me that he would be taking me on trips to places like Montego Bay. He just said, "Our bags are packed and we're taking a trip." I had never been on a plane before, so the experience of taking off, gliding through the air and feeling like I was floating on billowy clouds was pure bliss. Camron would order drinks for me since I wasn't of legal age. I got blitzed on the plane. In Cam's presence I felt so free and at ease. He was my savior. We talked intimately on the plane about things that really got on our nerves and about the things we loved to do. It made for a better ride, especially after a little turbulence unsteadied the plane. The pilot did an excellent landing job.

When we finally got to the airport and started removing our bags, I was anxious to see what all the other girls that had been to Montego Bay, Jamaica, were talking about. I wasn't feeling the shabby-looking airport. It wasn't like the Philadelphia airport at home. Ours was considered elegant compared to theirs. We stayed at an all-inclusive resort called *Mo' Bay*. Oh, I just loved it. Beautiful palm trees, white sand, pure blue water and a mid afternoon breeze that would put a child with Attention Deficit Disorder to sleep. The rooms were so well kept and decorated. Our room was a beachfront suite. This was the first time I ever stayed in a beachfront suite.

Camron definitely earned some points that day. At night the moon was positioned in such a way that it appeared to be sitting directly on the blue water. One night, Cam and I made love on the rooftop in the Jacuzzi while watching the moon. Those were the most incredible, intense orgasms I ever had. I was deeply infatuated with him after that night. The exposure to different lifestyles kept me in awe. I never wanted to return back to the boring life I once led.

Thankfully, the first trip wouldn't be our last. Jamaica was like a home away from home. We would visit Jamaica like we were going to New York. Once when we returned from Jamaica, we stayed in Brooklyn for a few days. Those few days were more exciting than any of our plane trips. The men in New York were so different. Most of them seemed so serious and business oriented, even in the drug game. That was astonishing to me. Most of the guys in Delaware hustled for cars, clothing, jewels and women. These guys were hustling for homes, future rap careers, producing music and opening stores with their own clothing lines. I realized that we thought so small compared to the Big Apple. I had future plans of opening a shoe store in downtown Wilmington— not any ol' shoe store, but one that had very sophisticated, playa-ristic original shoes; no two pairs would be alike. They would range from sizes made for infants to a size twelve for women and fourteen for men. Delaware only had a few good shoe stores, and those stores were in the major malls. I'd definitely make a killing off that venture. I'd call it *Precioustymes Feet Boutique.*

In New York I met Prince, a soldier in Camron's camp. Prince was a tall and handsome young man. He had a smile similar to Michael Jordan's. There was something about his smile that kept him fresh in my mind—even after the trip to New York.

One particular night, Camron took me to Daddy's House restaurant. The atmosphere was like no other place I'd ever been in, so, again, this was a first. Cam always kept me experiencing new things. I liked that about him. He was sweet when he wanted to be and a nasty mothafucka if you crossed him. If things didn't go his way, he would straight flip on your ass.

For example, one time he asked me to cook some fried chicken for dinner. I didn't want him to know I'd never been taught to cook, so I fronted like I was a five-star chef from a five- star restaurant. I went out to the grocery store and picked up several fresh packs of boneless chicken. I also picked up some garden fresh stringed beans, onions and red peppers. A few ladies in the grocery store were getting these same items, so I figured what the hell, I'd grab them too. Shopping for groceries made me feel like I belonged to a loving family. Living with my mama at my grandma's, I couldn't remember once going to a grocery store or supermarket. It was always, "Here, take these stamps and go over to the corner store and get a half a dozen of eggs, a quarter pound of American cheese and a dozen of those glazed donuts." Every Saturday, guaranteed, that was a ritual for my mother, although she never cooked for my brother and me—just for herself and whoever her man was at the time. And we had to practically beg to get a half of one of those blazing glazed donuts. For a long time, I thought the corner store was the grocery store. Diamond, one of the chicks from the Won Sumth'n Clique, had a mother just the opposite of mine.

The first time I realized that was when she invited me to spend the day with her and eat dinner at her house. We went to the store together, just like a family. I walked the aisles proudly, smelling the fresh fruits and vegetables, looking over the prices of all the snacks—Tasty Cakes, Chips Ahoy cookies, puddings, strawberry shortcake, all the good stuff. Her mom had a grocery cart full of food without food stamps! Diamond wasn't able to pull the wool over my eyes; she didn't belong in the streets. It was my background that mandated the streets for me. I would have given anything to be in her shoes.

When I finally got back to the condo from the supermarket, Cam wasn't there. I figured he had to make a run. That was cool because it gave me an opportunity to prepare the   meal without him hovering over me. I placed all the fresh poultry on the counter and ripped off the plastic covering it. I put the chicken in the sink and rinsed it off. I grabbed a bowl that I could use to flour the chicken. Searching the cabinets and pantry area, I realized that we were out of flour, and I had forgotten to pick some up from the store. It would have been easy for me to run out to the corner store, but there wasn't one in this neighborhood. What we did have was some corn meal. I figured that was a perfect substitute. I let the chicken sit in the corn meal and I added the onions and green peppers. When the oil in the pan got really hot, I placed four pieces of chicken in, along with the onions and peppers. In the meantime, I cleansed the fresh stringed beans and put them into a small pan.

The meal was going to be the bomb! We didn't have any butter, so I used a few drops of oil to coat the green beans. I'd purchased a new tablecloth for the special occasion. When all the chicken was fried, I set the table in preparation for dinner. Since this was my first time cooking, I purchased a cute little apron set—not the kind your grandma or your grandma's mother would wear, but a sexy little apron to set the mood. I wanted to make sure everything was right before Cam came home, so I took a quick shower. Soon after getting dressed, in walked Cam. I was so excited and eager for us to eat dinner like husband and wife.

At first I thought he was playing when he said, "What's that horrible smell in here?" I brushed it off, but when he sat down at the table, not even acknowledging my outfit or the hard work I put into cooking all the food, I started to get upset even though I didn't show it.

I fixed his plate and sat right in front of him with an ice-cold Pepsi. "Here, baby!" I said.

He took one look at the chicken and said, "What kind of fried chicken is this?"

"Just try it," I said.

He took one bite and spit it clear across the room. "Are you trying to poison me, bitch?" I was crushed—not only from him expressing his displeasure in the meal I had prepared, but for calling me a bitch like that. I observed his angry body language before going into the bedroom. He walked in the bedroom behind me and smacked me upside the head. "Did you hear me talking to you? That food is horrible. I ain't never had fried chicken that taste that bad. If you didn't know how to cook, you should have said something. It's not like we couldn't have had food delivered or gone out to a restaurant like we always do."

"But I wanted this dinner to be special for us, Cam."

"Yeah, it was special, all right—especially nasty!" he said brutally. I never cooked for him again after that. And it was then that I knew I had to get my money and soon bounce. Camron started to really get out of hand.

Chapter 5

Baby Mama Drama

Camron and I practically shared his condo—that is until his baby's mama came and interrupted our arrangement. She called and arrived the same day. Normally I would have detected her schemes way beforehand, but she caught me in a vulnerable state.

"Hello?" I answered very politely.

"Put Camron on the phone. It's an emergency."

"Who's calling?" I said, switching to defense mode.

"It's Nikki, his baby's mother." Her words were short and direct. I could tell she was from New York by her accent. "Is he there or what?" She asked again, apparently because I took too long to answer. "Kenny told me he had another flunky so I guess that's you," she said nonchalantly. "What's your name anyway? Is this the broke bitch from Delaware he cleaned up? Moved you from a shack to his condo. Imagine that! You must give a helluva blowjob!" She was straightforward, not holding back any information.

I gave the phone receiver a second look. *Who does this ho think she is?* "See, it's skanks like you who deserve the dial tone. I guess you'll talk to him some other time!" I said before hanging up. *See-ya! The nerve of that bitch...she must don't know who she's messing with.*

When Camron got out of the shower he asked who was on the line. I told him it was a prank caller as I dried off his back. I was not about to let her ruin my sweet situation, so I pushed her call to the back of my mind.

Looking at Camron just fresh out the shower, I couldn't resist the thought of his warm body pressing against mine. He had been working out on a daily, and just looking at his physique made my panties become moist. Pushing him against the wall, I couldn't help but drop to my knees to taste his beautiful love muscle.

She was right. I was good at putting my thing down. Before I knew it we were lying naked in the bed. His soft and gentle touch caressed every inch of my body. The thickness of his tongue between my inner thighs had my mind twisted. He gently licked and sucked my pearl until I let out screams of ecstasy. Immediately following my orgasms, he inserted his thick love shaft and went to work—twists, turns, from the back and from the side until he burst on the inside. Afterward we lay on the bed in each other's arms. There was no doubt in my mind that I was in love, lust or just plain dick-dizzy. This man had me!

Kenny didn't bother to knock on the bedroom door. He just busted right in. "Cam, Nikki is at the front gate." My eyes almost popped out of my head. At that point, I jumped out of bed 'cause I knew it was gon' be some shit.

"What the fuck does she want? When the hell did she get here?" he asked angrily.

"I don't know, but she said she called earlier and Mona hung up on her!" Kenny exclaimed. With a very disturbed look on his face, Cam asked me if I knew anything about what Kenny was saying.

"Well, the bitch did call but—"

He stopped me in my tracks. "I thought I told you about that shit. I don't care *who* it is or *who* you jealous of, when the phone rings for Cam, that's who it's for. Don't let it happen again, and don't think you're going to start no beef between Nikki and me. I don't need the drama, sweetheart!" His words cut me like a knife. I was like, what the fuck...*Nikki and me*...he said it like they were a couple. He glanced at himself in the mirror. "Kenny, go to the gate and sign her in."

I hurriedly cleaned up so her first impression of me would be one to remember. I took a seat in the front living room. This was unusual for me because normally I would relax in the den, but there was a better view of the entranceway from the living room.

Miss priss came strolling in with her high stilettos and a pair of low-rise jeans that exposed the crack of her ass. She stood almost six feet fall. She was the model type—light skin, small waist, long legs and a mean stride. I wasn't impressed, though; I had Camron and she didn't. As long as the dollars flowed, I didn't care.

"Where's my baby?" he asked her.

"She's back home with Granny. I came up to discuss some business with you—alone!" she said, glaring at me.

"Oh, I'm not going anywhere. This is my home, too!" I said, marking my territory.

"That's funny, I thought your little hood-ass lived in De-la-ware," she said with a sneer.

"Both of y'all cut the bullshit 'cause you're making me mad," Cam said with a discerning look on his face. I could see that he was growing uneasy, so I just let it go. After their discussion, Camron told me he wanted to talk with me. Kenny showed Nikki to the guestroom and told her that he'd get her bags from the trunk of the Mercedes 500 SL. Instead of taking her bags directly into the house, he kept them in the trunk of the car until Camron okayed her stay.

"Yes, we do need to talk," I said in a strong tone.

"Who the fuck do you think you are talking to?" Cam turned around and smacked me in the face. His tone was intimidating and strong.

I fell to the floor. "Oooh," I faintly moaned. My face felt like it had a big red hand printed on it. My heart was deeply bruised. I should've believed him when he said he'd be the only one hurting me.

"Get your ass in the room!" He kicked me square in the ass when I hurried by. I went without a word and lay across the bed quietly. "Nikki will be staying with us for a while, so get used to it. I suggest you two become good friends...if not, both of you bitches will be out in the street." My jaw dropped. I was stuck. I couldn't believe what was coming out of his mouth. "Now go and get dressed, 'cause I'm taking both of you to the mall, and afterwards we're going to a club on Delaware Avenue."

I knew I had to go along with the plan because if I didn't, I would have found myself back in Wilmington driving my little Honda again. I was not about to mess this up because of her. I had a plan, and nothing was going to get in the way of it.

If Nikki wanted war, war was what she was gon' get. She thought she had the upper hand because of her child, but that shit didn't mean anything to Camron. To him, pussy was pussy. A child had nothing to do with keeping a woman.

Nikki settled in the guest room as I watched her every move. My lips were so frowned up I could feel the tip of my nose. I wanted to go in the room and pounce on that trick. She had this snicker on her face like, *move over, bitch, cause Nikki is here!* I was about to prove this chick wrong. This was Mona's territory, and she had to play by my rules.

"Uh, um!" I made the sound loudly enough for her to turn my way. When she turned around, I gave her the finger. "Bitch!" I made sure to control the level of my voice so Cam wouldn't hear me.

She smiled and said, "Young girls."

"Oh, I got your young girl. Trust me, I do." After that, I got up and shut the bedroom door to get ready for our visit to the mall.

At the mall I didn't say a word. I just scanned around the stores for the most expensive and sexiest outfits I could find. Though she was taller than me, Nikki's body still couldn't touch mine. The look of envy was on every man's face as we strutted through the mall with Camron. Looking from the outside you would have thought that we were the happiest threesome on the planet; however, there was much internal strife among us.

It wouldn't have been so bad if Camron hadn't added fuel to the fire by holding both our hands. Even when we stopped to get something to eat, people were staring. Cam ordered food for all of us at Ruby Tuesdays. The waitress was friendly, but why shouldn't she have been, since Cam was flirting with her right in front of the both of us. Neither Nikki nor I dared to say anything with about ten bags apiece placed all around us, taking up additional customer seating. But on one of the waitress's many trips to our table, the looks that we both gave her were enough to make her appearances a lot scarcer.

Cam had a little sauce from his chicken on his face and I used my napkin to slightly dab it away.

"There you go, baby," I said, still feeding his ego even after he smacked the hell out of me. Nikki sighed and picked up a french fry and fed it to him. I had to blow the steam out past my shoulders. She was trying to outdo me. Okay, she was up one, but I managed to fuck her up with this next move: the table we sat at was U-shaped, so Cam sat in the middle; we were side by side with him. The attention was already on us. I picked up the bell to make a *ding-ding* sound to do a toast. Everyone in the room had their eyes planted on us. "Listen up, everyone, I'd like to make a toast to my man—the best man I've every had!" I lifted one of the mouthwatering strawberries from my plate and began feeding it to Cam from my mouth. The little hot-ass waitress said, "Oh, my, that's a little much for *Ruby Tuesdays!*"

Nikki got up from the table and pranced to the bathroom. I knew she was hot but I wasn't mad at her. I wasn't trying to be petty, but I had to let her know I am *that chick!* Don't mess with me if you ain't ready! And that night she wasn't. I turned it out at dinner and then later on at the club. I wore my red Chanel halter one-piece cat suit with my Chanel silver and red slides that Cam bought earlier that day. Nikki wore her new black Prada skirt set with her black and red stilettos sandal boots. They were cute, but she wasn't even on my level! Cam and Kenny posted up at the bar and bought drinks for everyone. The club was live, packed wall to wall with black folks, so you know I had to show out. I walked down to the dance floor and slid directly in front of the mirrors. Guys kept asking me to dance with them but I chose to dance by myself. Camron glancing my way every five seconds influenced my choice. Nikki was acting stuck-up, sitting alone at a table sipping on a drink. No one was paying her any attention. I was enjoying myself. They all flocked around to watch me. I danced like I was on a stage performing for a crowd of fans. *I like it when you do that right there!* Chingy, the rapper, repeated his words: *I like it when you do that right there! Lick your lips when you talking to me star!* I licked my lips and swayed my hips from side to side. Cam and all the men at the bar watched me closely as I *backed it up and let it drop!* I made Cam recognize that I was that chick. In his mind he knew this. That night Cam slept in the bedroom with me, cuddling and caressing my smooth skin. I should've never acted up like that earlier, because after that night he acted like a deranged fool every time he was with me. That *snap-back-come-back* of mine wasn't to be taken lightly!

Chapter 6

The Switch

After a while, having Nikki around didn't even bother me. I got used to having miss priss on the scene. I had the upper hand and Cam slept in my bedroom every night. Nikki's bed stayed on chill. The money was still fluent and not only did we have the black Mercedes 500SL, a bronze Grand Jeep Cherokee and a black Lexus LS400, but we had a burgundy Hummer H2. I didn't have to work and school was far from my mind. This could have gone on for eternity, but it wasn't Cam's plan.

"You lazy-ass bitches better get up and find some type of employment. I'm tired of seeing you just lounge around the house watching television shows all day. Neither one of you is trying to better yourself. This shit ain't always going to be around. Stop depending on me! Nikki, when was the last time you spent time with our daughter? You've been here for six months and Granny still has her. You aren't doing shit."

"Well, I don't see you spending time with her, either," she replied. Before she could finish her last word, he jumped on her. I froze. He was beating the shit out of her. I even felt sorry for her but I didn't say a word, thinking I might be next. I even knew better not to stare too long or show sympathy, fearing what Cam might do to me.

"You want to talk back, slut! All the shit I do for you and Mya...Granny doesn't want for nothing. Who purchased her home? Who bought her car? Who sends her $2500 weekly for her bills? Who spits out cash for our daughter? Don't you spend my money at the malls? Don't you drive nice cars? Don't you travel at my expense? I do all these things, you ungrateful bitch! You don't do shit! Now, go get your shit. I'm taking your trick-ass back to New York today. *Mona!* " He screamed my name so loudly that I was almost too frightened to move.

I replied softly. "Yes?"

"You get dressed, too. You're going with me."

I was uncertain what he had in mind, because with him it was always hard to tell. I just followed the directions. Nikki was crying hysterically, begging him to forgive her. He wasn't trying to hear a word she was saying. I knew that once anyone crossed him or started being ungrateful, they were a done deal. I had to make sure I didn't blow my chances!

Cam drove the Hummer H2. Kenny followed in the LS400. I drove the Cherokee with Nikki as the passenger. In the jeep she finally calmed down and wanted to talk sensibly.

"You know, you really should leave him," she whispered as if he could hear us.

"Look, Nikki, let's get one thing straight. We were never friends from the start. I sympathize with you, right now, but uh, you should have kept your mouth shut. You know how he can be."

"Cam doesn't love me, you or anybody else for that matter. He's out for himself," she snapped.

"Well, he's been good to me."

"Yeah, but look what you put up with, Mona. He sleeps with any woman willing to give up the ass, and he doesn't use protection. You know that as well as I do, because we both had gonorrhea three times or more in the last six months. Aren't you afraid of contracting HIV?" She was absolutely right, but the lifestyle Camron was providing me with was far from the one I was used to. I had a plan. I needed Cam to finance *Precioustymes Feet Boutique*. It would be tough but I was determined. I wasn't going to put up with all kinds of shit—for nothing! I could certainly get past Cam's infidelity—for something!

"Okay, you made a valid point, but how many of them sluts get to live, drive, get money and dress the way we do? Those chicks are on the streets tricking, stripping or selling his dope. Have you ever had to do any of those things? Besides, gonorrhea is curable. What's one shot in the ass from time to time. I mean, come on, bitches are fighting for him on the streets. You've been the only drama I've faced since being with him, and that's only because you have his daughter. Otherwise, I wouldn't have even encountered you, trick!" In my mind, I knew what I said had made no sense at all, but I didn't want her really knowing how I felt internally.

"What about your morals and values?" she asked. "You're not making sense, Mona."

"Fuck morals and values. That's for the old heads. This shit is real life, Nikki! What is it that you don't get? Just be glad you can go back and live with your granny off of his money. I don't have anyone to turn to, so you can preach that shit to the next bitch."

Normally, I wouldn't have thought twice about what I had just said, but inside I hurt deeply. All my morals and respect were lost when Cam took control of me. I never bothered calling home to see how my moms or grandma was doing. I hadn't talked to any of my friends in months.

"One day you will wake up," she said frowning. "And hopefully before it's not too late."

"So, I guess you suddenly woke up today just before he put your ass out!" I screamed.

"Mona, you don't know Cam like I know him."

"Well, I know him well enough to know not to be an ungrateful bitch like you."

"Listen to me, Mona, and hear me out, please! I know you're probably wondering why Cam hasn't introduced you to his family with the exception of Kenny, right? I bet he didn't tell you he had two other brothers and a sister in Brooklyn, did he?" She was right. He never said a word about his family other than Kenny, but what was her point? Beside the business, I really didn't know anything about him.

"About a year ago, Cam's mom was murdered by his father. At the time, he was in Rikers on a first-degree murder charge. He was later released due to evidence tampering by the N.Y.P.D. He was furious with his brothers and sister for not addressing their father before things got out of control. His brothers were sixteen and eighteen, and his sister was fourteen years old. Age didn't make a difference to him. He taught the game to them early and blamed them for not keeping their moms safe while he was away. He was the protector of the family and felt his pops should have been killed before he had a chance to kill their moms. However, Cam accidentally shot and killed his pop's friend during his attempt to kill his father. That's why he went to Rikers on the first-degree murder charge. He knew shit was going to escalate after he went away, and he begged his moms to leave, even giving her $500,000 to relocate.

"His mom was a God-fearing woman, trying to create a holy environment for her children. She spent many days down at the Shiloh Worship Temple on Saratoga and served on every committee formed. Mrs. Shug was known as a respected church mother and committee leader. Although she made a strong appearance in the church, her home life suffered tremendously from neglect. Her sacrifice to attend church services caused her relationship with her children to slowly diminish. She became a woman practicing religion and pleasing the pastor instead of concentrating on building her family. Her children never attended church with her except on Easter, and that was only because she 'd be there all day. During the sermon they were always talking, sometimes throwing bibles from pew to pew, causing her embarrassment. Nights when she was preoccupied at the church, her husband, Jab, in a sick fit, would beat and torment the children—especially Cam and Kenny since they were not his biologically.

"Jab performed petty jobs like collecting cans, selling copper pipes and cleaning cars, and he was known most recently as the *Window Washer King*; so Cam started hustling at eleven years old and Kenny at twelve. On any given day, Jab knew that Kenny or Cam had at least a hundred dollars in their possession. The drama always began with the same questioning.

" 'Which one of you lil' niggas got some doe? Don't lie to me, either, or I'll wrap this cable cord around your neck, you little punk-ass, snotty-nose mothafuckas! Give the doe

up!' "

When they didn't respond he would cold pop them right in the face, back and forth. Kenny's knees would buckle after every hit, and he'd fall to the ground and assume a fetal position. Cam would stand there bucking with all his strength and grit like a raging bull after being hit.   Kenny feared Jab and would give up his hard-earned, weeklong hustling money of a hundred dollars every time. Cam was persistent and never gave his up. He was wiser than his older brother. Instead of giving Jab doe, he would supply him with his need. He started giving him balloon-filled balls of heroin. That was even better 'cause Jab hated going out to cop, and the dope Cam was getting was considered top notch and far better than what they were selling down on Fulton Street directly across from Shiloh Worship Temple, the church his wife attended. This way he didn't risk being exposed by one of the nosy-ass church members. His dope was delivered right to his apartment. Things didn't start to go badly until Cam and Kenny got older and moved into an apartment of their own. That's when the abuse shifted to Mrs. Shug and the three younger siblings. Meanwhile, the streets absorbed Cam and Kenny. Street life was what they knew best and represented. Street hustlers were who they were. Local niggas, rap niggas and sports figures became very respectful of their *gangsta*.

"Trying to forget about the past after they moved out, they struggled to overlook Jab's former abuse, but after many visits to the church to see their mother, they noticed that she continuously had a black eye—sometimes two. After the third or fourth time, it was on. Jab took many a beating from his stepsons. Since

Jab was a former boxing semi-pro, they always left with a slit eye or swollen lip. Not giving up, they continued to whip his ass until receiving bloody satisfaction on each occurrence. That was never enough for Cam, though; he wanted Jab six feet under laying deep in a body bag. Kenny was satisfied with a beat down every week.

"Fortunately for Jab, both Kenny and Cam got knocked messing around with this Haitian chick named Treaty—Kenny for two trafficking charges and Cam for an attempted murder charge. Cam told Kenny not to fuck with Treaty on several occasions, 'cause she was from the gritty Flatbush area known for setting dudes up. Those tricking-ass busters weren't to be fucked with, but Kenny was soft when it came to a piece of ass.

After eight months on the inside, Cam and Kenny found themselves attending their mother's funeral. After taking so many beat downs her body became weary. She didn't have the strength or energy to take cover one afternoon when Jab blindly struck her on the side of her head. Her body stumbled, finding its way to a sharp-edged radiator. That was the last blow she would ever take. Cam was outraged and plotted on revenge. He demanded that his lawyer work overtime on his case until the day of his release.

Luckily for him, he was released due to a mistrial, but Kenny wasn't so lucky; he remained locked up for another year. Cam was already slightly mentally challenged. This tragedy sent him into a realm of darkness. He became untouchable, having a heart of stone with black blood running through his veins.

"As a God-fearing woman, Miss Shug wanted no parts of the dirty money that Camron had offered her. She told him that God would take care of her. She had no idea that her husband had fallen prey to heroine. Had she not spent so much time in church she may have noticed the signs. Instead, she attended church services regularly. Her strong determination to get her sons off the streets was revealed in her prayers, and she had plenty of faith in the Lord. Her only weakness was her jealous, deranged, dope-addicted husband.

"Out of the blue one-day, Cam appeared in front of the projects. No one except him and his lawyer knew that his case was overturned. He crept up on Prospect Plaza in a delirious state of mind, his hat pulled very low and dressed in army fatigues. Those that knew him from around the hood knew he was up to something. No one dared to acknowledge his presence. When he arrived on the seventeenth floor of the high-rise-building, he quietly slipped inside the apartment like he was on a mission to rob a stranger. He never gave the evil spirit lurking   inside his body a second thought because his younger brothers and sisters represented the blood that ran through Jab's veins.

"At the time, his two brothers and sister were sitting in the apartment plotting to kill their father. Just as soon as he appeared, he pointed two Mac-10's directly at his younger brothers. As one of them tried to escape, everyone on the seventeenth floor could hear his sister's roars and sobs. It was as if a demon took over him. He was totally out of control. With a horrifying look of disdain, he questioned them about how they could allow their mother to die and not retaliate. He didn't give them a chance to respond; he just blasted round after round until the last bit of life lay still on the floor. To make sure everyone was dead, he stood over each body and delivered one last bullet to each head. No one in the apartment complex bothered to call the police until the foul smell of decay was too unbearable. The reason Kenny was spared was because he was in prison.

"The sad part is that he arranged and paid for a combined funeral for them all. The day after the funeral, he fled New York following Controversy on tour for a little over a year until Kenny was released.

Controversy never agreed, but he also didn't disagree, fearing Cam would kill him as well."

I sat dumbfounded. I was dealing with a cold-hearted killer, straight like that and had no idea what I was in for.

"Cam rented out that condo in Philly as a hiding spot until things calmed down. I would've been living in the condo, but he didn't want me to make any sudden moves. I don't know how you became a permanent fixture on his side. Normally, you would have been fucked and left alone. For some reason he's keeping you around; so pay close attention to his motives. Camron is a notorious murderer! I want you to know this because sooner or later he will kill you and me. And another thing, Camron is not his birth name—Alexander King is... never, ever mention that! He will kill you."

"I don't understand. Nikki, if you know all these things, why haven't you contacted the police?"

"Bitch, are you dumb! He has Brooklyn, Newark, New Jersey, and Philly on lock! Don't underestimate him...he has police officers on his payroll. This shit is larger than you think. With your naive Delaware mentality, you will be eaten alive. All your dumb ass can see is the materialistic things. There are other ways to get them beside this. However, it's too late for you to turn back now. You're in it for the ride, so wise up quick to the game the Brooklyn way! This shit is serious!"

Though I didn't let her see it, I was petrified. From the look on her face, she wasn't joking, and I was scared for my life! For the rest of the ride we rode in silence. I never questioned her about what she told me. I was too busy thinking about what the hell I was going to to do. We didn't so much as turn and look at each other after that until we reached our destination.

It was still questionable if I should believe her. Cam could be a little violent and nasty at times, but I couldn't fathom him killing his own family. Maybe this was a ploy she was using to lure me out of the picture. I mean, why should I trust her?

When Cam got out of the car, he summoned Nikki to stay put as he walked toward Granny's house. We both sat stiffly, constantly staring out the window wondering what would come next.

After about forty-five minutes, he came out and walked to the passenger's side of the car. He said, "Listen up, ma, Granny and I think it's best that you stay somewhere else other than her house, so I'll be taking you to Kiesha's where you'll stay and make some money for a change. However, you are to make sure that every Friday, all proceeds with the exception of fifty bucks, gets placed in Kiesha's hands by six o'clock p.m. Otherwise, you will answer to me. You understand that!" he said, grabbing her face.

I was in total disbelief. Nikki and I both knew that Kiesha's house was the trick house. That's where all the tricks, ballers and gamblers went for sales, dice games, packages and to get their dicks sucked and a quick fuck.

Nikki was crying uncontrollably as Camron continued on. "Now, to make sure you don't pull a fast one, Mona is going to stay with Granny until further notice."

"What!" I screamed. "Cam, but I don't even know Granny. The only thing I knew about Granny was that she was Nikki's grandmother and kept Nikki's daughter, Mya. She didn't call to the house and rarely did we go to visit. In fact, this *was* my first visit to her house. Granny respected Cam, I don't know why. Maybe it was because of the money. Then again, it couldn't have been that. She was a Christian woman, and most Christians didn't accept dirty drug money.

I'd seen a few pictures of her and Mya at the condo. She was short and fat, with beautiful black and silver curly hair. Her eyes had worry bags under them. In all the pictures she wore a different housecoat. There was one with her and Mya at Easter time. She was dressed to kill in a badass, yellow outfit. Pointless to say, I still was a stranger to her.

"You didn't know me, either, when your trick ass decided to move in with me, did you?" he replied. "You tricks done had your fair share. Nikki turned and looked at me as if to say, "I told you so." I wanted to cry but I had to maintain my composure.

"Mona, I don't know what you look like you're getting ready to cry for. Word to mother, I could place you in Kiesha's, too, but I have something else planned for you. This time, I'll cut you some slack. You can still keep the Cherokee. I'll make sure you get a weekly allowance of a thousand dollars. Your job is to make sure that my daughter and Granny are protected from this evil bitch!"

I wanted to yell out, "Nigga, I'm not scared of you and I wouldn't even dare let you see me in a weak state...Nikki's the weakling, not me!" But the words never left my lips.

How could he have managed to hate Nikki so much in one day? She had to have done more for him to act like this. "Now, get the fuck out of the car and go inside to introduce yourself to Granny before I change my mind!" he said to me. Then he stared directly at Nikki and said, "Let's go, you little ungrateful bitch. You're coming with me." He had to literally pull her from the car because she was holding onto the seat so tightly, kicking and screaming.

"Noooo! Please Cam, no!" she screamed in agony. When he finally yanked her out of the car, a clump of her hair was left behind, stuck in the closed door. I watched in horror. Before throwing her into his vehicle, he repeatedly delivered blows to her head and face, causing his hands to become covered with blood. Then he reached into his trunk and pulled out a pair of handcuffs to cuff her to the back seat. By now she was unconscious.

Chapter 7

Fifth The Forklift

Cam continued his operations as usual, collecting his money and making his rounds. He made it his business to keep a close watch on Yatta because of the situation with me. Just to be sure I hadn't made contact with my family, phones at Granny's were tapped, so if I were up to something grimy, he would deal with me before it surfaced.

He rode to Delaware to Fifth and Madison on the Westside to look for Yatta. The night was so live. It seemed as if there was a block party going on. Music was blasting from parked cars and the niggas were huddled in packs everywhere smoking trees. Chicks were dressed provocatively; either in see-through halter dresses showing imprints of thongs or low-rise shorts showing hips and ass. Most of them were just waiting for a chance to seduce a hustler before the night wore out. The fiends were coming from all angles and hustlers were moving steadily, trying to make money.

Camron parked the Hummer H2 and Prince parked the LS400 behind Seventh and Jefferson. They all walked confidently down to Fifth and Madison where he spotted Yatta playing C-Lo with about fifteen dudes. One of the guys playing C-lo noticed the new faces. He gestured to Yatta and asked, "Who the fuck these niggas posted up on our block like they running shit?"

"Yo, chill B," Yatta said calmly. "That's Cam and them. Y'all stay put for a minute. What up, Cam?"

"Let me talk to you for a minute, son." His New York Yankees fitted hat was pulled down almost covering his eyes. Across the street from Fifth Street sat the Hicks Anderson Community Center where most of the youngsters hung out. They were watching over the railing to see if any physical action was going to go down.

"Yo, the last time we met up I fronted you two kilos, and I only collected $22,000 from one of your niggas. My man, you need to get your troops in order before you have to deal with me—or deal with these niggas!" He motioned toward the seven guys standing across the street. "I'll be back next week to collect another $22,000, plus $5,000 in interest for making me wait a week and being late."

Without holding his tongue, Yatta quickly responded. "Hold up, man, which nigga fell short?" Most of my niggas always come through. Just point him out. As a matter of fact, I'm gon' do it."

Yatta wasn't scared of Cam or his crew. On the Forklift they had just as many guns as Cam—thanks to Cam. Yatta whistled to get his crew's attention. They knew when Yatta whistled like that something was wrong. They came from all directions, ready to get down. Everyone was present except for Darryl. "Any of these niggas look familiar to you?" asked Yatta. The situation had to be dealt with immediately before he found himself at war with these New York motherfuckers.

"Look, nigga, I don't have time to stand around while you get your house in order. Just make sure you got my money next week, straight like that, or you can forget about the next shipment until we settle this shit." And with that, he walked off.

Yatta was hot. Without his connection, he couldn't move weight. He could've copped from the next man, but Cam had top quality and the best prices. Yatta paced up and down the street showing his anger. "If any one of you niggas is holding back information on me, you better let that shit go now; otherwise, you will find yourself right next to Darryl's stiff dead ass after I catch up to him!"

Coming up with $22,000 wasn't a problem for Yatta. His problem was the weakling causing havoc in the game. He didn't want Cam to think that he was the one holding back.

Chapter 8

Betrayal

After settling in at Granny's, I actually felt safe being away from Camron. She had a beautiful home in Manhattan overseeing the Hudson River. I became particularly fond of one of the three and a half bathrooms. Two fourteen-carat, gold-stained glass doors were what did it. Inside was a his-and-hers vanity made with a marble burgundy counter top. The floor was covered with marble burgundy floor tile, which accented the countertop perfectly. There was a huge sunken heart-shaped Jacuzzi with five gold spiral steps. Since the marble pattern in the countertop and floor tile were gold, the gold spiral steps gleamed. There were two toilets and one shower. Cam had the artwork in this bathroom imported from

Italy. Even the gold crystal chandelier was imported.
It was more than beautiful; it was breathtaking. You
could easily   relax in this bathroom; it was the size of
two bedrooms combined. This was where I spent most
of my time. I started a daily journal to waste away my
days.

 Dear Diary,

 *You know what, for a young woman my age that
sounds so corny, so let me flip it.*

 Dear Journal,

 *Yeah, that sounds better. I guess things are going
as expected in my life. Cam is not really what I expected.
But what did I really expect from a hustler? I know he
has some feelings for me, but I know not the feelings I
deserve. He got me living over old-timer-ass Granny's
house. She acts all funny, like she doesn't want to talk
to me. She even keeps little cute Mya away. I know the
little girl has to be bored, living with her great
grandmother. Nikki and Cam need to stop living like
they don't have a child. That shit is real crazy, just
leaving your child like that. I wonder if Nikki is really
tricking up in Kiesha's or if they trying to play me—
seems odd that he would make his baby's mama go
trick in a whorehouse. I wonder if my mama is still
tripping off them men. I bet just like Nee, she's
somewhere with her nose stuck up their ass! Well at*

least I have better living conditions. I can leave whenever I want to, well, to get my hair done, a manicure a pedicure or to the grocery store. What's so bad about that? All right, this ain't even me! What the hell am I doing? I could be back on Westside working some nigga for some loot, right now! But why would I do that when they can't provide for me this life that I'm living with Cam? It's really not so bad. I wonder what's up with Controversy's fine ass. I would love to bump into him on a rainy day, sunny day, stormy day, shit whatever day! Well, I'll chit-chat later. I'm about to lay up in this Jacuzzi and act like I'm that chick! Till next time... Precioustymes!

It was like living in a dream. It was far from my days of sleeping on a plastic-covered couch. I was able to sleep peacefully through the night. For the life of me, I couldn't understand why Nikki would leave this surrounding to live in Philly. Cam would have never heard a word from me. She had the life many women struggled for. Word! What was the problem?

After what Nikki had told me, I wanted to be far away from Cam. He was right. I had my fair share of his company but not his money. I was contemplating driving back to Delaware and putting all this behind me. I wasn't really scared, but sometimes I wasn't sure what direction Cam was coming from. However, since I'd allowed my mom to move into my apartment and keep the car, I decided against going home.

What would the girls think of me if I came home now? Many of them admired me, but there were many that hated, too. Fuck it. I was going to do me. I wouldn't dare give them the satisfaction of coming home broke. Unh-huh, no way in hell! I made it too far to go back like that. I thought that maybe I'd go back after stashing my cash.

Even though I was in a safe haven, there were times I didn't feel at home around Granny, and I was now seeing for myself what she had probably put Nikki through.

Granny and I never talked. I felt so alone in her house. It was obvious that she was uneasy about the living arrangements even though she never expressed it. The only time she said anything to me was during dinner. Dinnertime was the only time I wasn't alone. I spent it with Mya, Camron and Nikki's daughter. She was the sweetest and most adorable little girl to be around. Her eyes were wide and beautiful. She had long, pretty ponytails and Shirley Temple curls. How could they both neglect her?

Every Friday, one of Camron's lieutenants, named Prince, would come to the house to pick up Granny and Mya. Before they left, they always went up to Granny's room. The only time I'd see Mya smile was when Prince came around. Prince would seldom speak, fearing that I'd tell Cam. I was labeled off limits to all of his crew.

Neither one of them kept me informed on where they were going or why they had to secretly meet in Granny's room. I figured it most likely had something to do with them going to a neutral location to meet Nikki, so she could spend time with Mya. That was cool with me because it gave me a chance to inspect some things in the house.

Being in solitude helped me to build back up my confidence and character. I put my game face back on. Every Friday when they left, I would thoroughly examine one of the five bedrooms, keeping notation of what each room contained. I even jotted down the time they left and the minute they came back, which was two hours and forty-five minutes every Friday around noon. I noticed that every room had a treasure chest and a safe—all which remained locked. I would check every Friday to see if Granny would slip up and leave at least one of them unlocked. How lucky was I when she left the safe and treasure chest in her bedroom unlocked one afternoon. Without hesitation, I opened the treasure chest. It was stacked with bundles of crisp one-hundred-dollar bills. I estimated that there was at least $500,000 inside. The safe contained a money market statement with the names *Nancy Johnson* and

Mya Brown printed on it. The account balance read *$1,500,000*. I blinked my eyes to get a better focus. It read the same. Time was passing quickly, and I realized that in fifteen minutes they would be back. It also contained birth records for Nikki, Mya and a man named

Drew Moore. *Who was Nancy Johnson and why was she the overseer of Mya's account? Why did Granny have this statement? Who the hell was Drew Moore?* The more I searched the more I wanted to find out. I paid close attention to the fact that Mya's birth record did not list the father's name. *Why hadn't Nikki put Cam's name on Mya's birth certificate?*

Inside were also three rings of keys. I imagined that at least one set would open the other treasure chests and safes. Glancing quickly again at my watch I realized that my time was up. Damn! They would be arriving in less than three minutes. I carefully placed the documents and the keys, with the exception of one set, back into the safe. I knew that at any moment they would come through the door.

Hopefully, Granny wouldn't notice that a set of keys was missing. Seeing all that money made me want to go for mine. Shit, I'm sure a couple of stacks of those crisp bills wouldn't be missed at all.

I crept silently into my bedroom and lay across my bed as if I was napping the whole time. When I heard the door shut, I took a peek to see if Prince had come in. He had, and he was looking fine as ever in his deep navy blue suit.

Summer months had come to an end and the fall season was well under way. Trees in the area were full of beautiful reddish yellow leaves that colorfully brightened the day. The cheerfulness of the season began to set the slut in me free. Besides, I was horny as hell. I hadn't been hit off in a while and I was tired of masturbating. My *Pearl Panther* vibrator died last week from me wearing that thing out! You should have seen the look on Granny's face when my novelty order came c.o.d. from Precioustymes & *Then* Sum Entertainment. She was all flustered in the face after reading the bold writing: *FOR ADULT PLEASURE ONLY!*

My lustful spirit was growing stronger by the day. And today, I was bold enough to express myself, no matter what the consequences. "Hey, Prince!" I said very seductively from the top of the stairs. The way Granny cut her eyes at me I should've been sliced in two. "Let her look on," I thought, as I called his name again. This time she wore a look of disgust. "I know you heard me, Prince. Can I have a few moments of your time? Well, since you want to ignore me, your boss called while you were out, and he told me to pass on some information." On that note, Granny disappeared and Prince headed up the steps to my bedroom. They would become very attentive whenever Cam's name was mentioned. Using this technique I never went wrong.

Once in my bedroom, I summoned Prince to close the door. "Look, I'm not for no games, ma!"

"Neither am I, poppy," I said smiling. There was a king-sized, mahogany bed in my room. A fluffy, white, feather down comforter along with two over-sized pillows covered it.

"What do you want?" he asked.

"A chance to get to know you—find out what I can do for you?"

"Look, girl, what message do you have for me?"

"Come closer and I'll tell you," I said playfully. His facial expression let me know he wasn't the least bit aroused or interested in personal conversation. "All right, all right, let me stop playing. You don't have to be this serious. Have a little fun once in awhile. To tell you the truth, I haven't heard from Cam since the day he left me here." Prince immediately started walking toward the door.

"Wait! Allow me to finish. This is a beautiful home and all...I feel very privileged to be here, but I am so lonely. I know he told you I was off limits, but I mean, every once in a while, maybe you can show a sista some love. Help me to adjust to this way of living."

He looked at me blankly and asked, "Are you done?" I was crushed.

"What the hell you mean am I done? Cam got your balls held that tight? What, you need his permission to piss as well? Attention...at ease soldier!" I was clowning him the best way I knew how.

By the time I gave him my final salute, he grabbed me and threw me down onto the bed. He ripped my blouse off, exposing my silver La Perla bra, and unzipped my pants. I loved it. "See, now, that's what I'm talkin' 'bout. I knew you had it in you," I said.

"Is this what you want?" he said, almost growling.

"This is exactly what I want," I hissed. I didn't even take offense to him grabbing me violently. His kisses were gentle but his presence was strong. I started taking off his shirt and unbuckling his pants. After removing his clothes, I stepped back to observe what I needed to prepare for. His penis was thick and oversized. A soft moan escaped my lips. He didn't say a word as he pulled down my pants and revealed my silver La Perla thong.

"That's right, take a good look. This may be the only chance you get to be with a real man," he said confidently. There it was, his breaking point! I knew it was on, then. Without wasting another second, we both betrayed the boss.

Dear Journal,

You would not believe what the hell my crazy ass did today. Remember that dude, Prince, who I met a while ago? Yeah, yeah, Cam's boy. He came to Granny's today and I couldn't resist him. He was looking damn good and the zipper on his pants told me he had a rather large package underneath! Ya heard me! Cam is playing. He must be laid up with another chick, but that's cool, 'cause I was laid up with his main man today. It was all love. I know Prince enjoyed it, too, the way he was moaning and all. What, you don't know? I got that bomb azz shizz! Aahhh...that snap-back-come-back shizz! Let me stop acting dumb. I'm tripping like this journal is really a person I'm communicating with when I'm really talking to myself! That's real crazy too! I'm getting ready to go to bed. I'm still a little sore, but that bubble bath has put me in relax mode, and my eyes are getting heavy. Till next time... Precioustymes!

Chapter 9

Suspicion Arises

Camron had plans on meeting with Felix, a heavy hitter from Peru, to arrange for his monthly delivery of two hundred kilos—a hundred of which he paid straight cash for and the other hundred on consignment. He called Prince to inform him of the delivery time. Prince showed no remorse since sleeping with me. His reaction to Camron was the same as always. Camron would've never thought that he would ever over-step his boundary with him.

"How are my baby girl and Granny?" Camron asked.

"No disrespect, Baby Pa, but you really need to pay them a visit," he responded, showing little fear.

"Yeah, I guess you're right. It's been a minute since I've been over there." Taking it a step further, Prince asked Cam if he had spoken to me. Without hesitation, Cam, while softly biting on a toothpick, slowly turned his head, and with a merciless look on his face said, "Nigga, what did you just ask me?"

"My man, you dropped the girl off two months ago and never looked back," he said.

"Whatever the fuck I do with my women is what I do with my women! You heard me! You may want to reconsider what you just said, because I'm feeling a bit disrespected."

"No disrespect, Pa, I'm just looking out for your best interest. Are you sure you can trust the chick?" Prince flipped it real quick.

"Oh, for a minute I thought you were feeling her," Cam said. "I know how she loves attention. I'm thinking you may be her next mark."

Prince looked Camron directly in the eyes and said, "I would never cross you."

"That's my nigga," Cam replied as he gave his main man some dap.

After dropping Prince off, Camron came to see Mya, Granny and me. What Prince said had really gotten under his skin. As he approached the driveway he noticed me staring coldly out of my bedroom window. When I realized it was Cam, I hurried up and closed the vertical blinds. With much agitation, Cam unlocked the front door and Mya came running out of nowhere. She must have smelled him coming. "Daddy! Daddy!" she screamed, jumping in his arms.

"How's my baby girl?"

"All smiles since seeing you," Granny interrupted. "Come in here, I need to talk with you." Granny moved quickly before he got too preoccupied with Mya. They turned and walked into the kitchen.

By now I was standing near the kitchen with my ears burning like hot coal. I didn't know what Granny was going to say or if she knew that after the Friday trips, Prince would sneak up to my room to hit me off.

Granny sat Cam down and proceeded to speak when I rushed into the kitchen to greet them. "Well, well, mister man—long time no see. I missed you, did you miss me?" I was really sounding cocky. "Of course you did, that's why I haven't heard from you in about two months."

Cam removed Mya from his lap and excused himself from the kitchen, pulling me by the shoulder. "Don't you ever in your life question me like that in front of my daughter!" He dragged me all the way to my bedroom and shoved me to the floor. "Get up, trick, I guess the situation with Nikki didn't phase you at all. Be glad I'm in a good mood today." I lay still, afraid of what his next move might be. "Get up, girl, and put on a jean outfit and a pair of your stilettos. Wear that matching rhinestone belt that hangs down over your hips. Put on one of those sexy thong shits— one that exposes your ass when you bend over!"

He couldn't deny that I was sexy as shit, and after seeing me he wanted to show me off. "I want you to take a ride with me. Don't be scared, I'm not taking you to Kiesha's," he laughed. His real thought was keeping me close after Prince's speculation.

Gaining a little heart, I stood up and said, "Why would you do that? I'm your most obedient woman. It's cool to finally get out and be amongst the living. You know I wouldn't go anywhere without you—of course, only to get my hair did."

Cam was a little skeptical about me. Everyone else thought I had his heart. You would've never known it from the way he treated me at times.

"So, where are we going?" I asked.

"We're taking a ride, that's all you need to know. Get dressed and be ready in twenty minutes. Oh, yeah, I'm going to talk with Granny. Make it your business to stay occupied," Cam said, looking directly at me. Shutting the door behind him, he called out to

Granny. "Granny, baby, I'm coming!" Granny was now relaxing in the family room. "Where's Mya?"

"I laid her down for a nap," Granny responded, laying back in her favorite recliner. Granny's tastes were very basic. She didn't like all the lavish gifts and furnishings. She did enjoy gospel plays from time to time, though, and sometimes she would bring a few of her friends over to play Bingo. During her game, I'd better not come downstairs for nothing. She didn't want any of them knowing who I was and why I was staying in her house. See, that's what I didn't get. Granny was a Christian woman, playing Bingo and card games and accepting money from a drug dealer. She even laundered it, but she still managed to have a problem with me. Sometimes I wondered if she was just mad because Nikki wasn't there. Maybe she thought I was taking her granddaughter's place.

"What do you need to talk to me about? Please don't tell me it's about that Mona?"

"Child, please," Granny responded. "That girl is scared to make a phone call, much less do something stupid. And she's the only child I know that takes two to three baths per day," she laughed. "I don't pay that girl no mind. She's no child of mine and I don't care if she drowns herself or not."

"Come on, Granny, that's no way for a Christian woman to be talking," said Cam.

"Maybe you are right about that, but I don't care for her little conniving behind. You know I'm not going to hold my tongue. If she says anything out of line, I'm going to let her   have it."

"You know I would never let her disrespect you. There's no question about that."

Making the smile on her face less obvious, she calmly said to him, "It's time to bring Nikki back home. Mya misses her dearly and God knows Nikki misses her. I believe you can trust her now."

"You think so?" Cam said. Granny, I know she's your blood, your grandbaby and all, but she's an ungrateful little—"

"Don't you say that out your mouth, boy, at least not in my presence. Now be respectful!"

"No disrespect intended. I'm sorry, Granny."

"Now, yes, I believe she's had ample time to steal from you and to escape, but she's remained true".

"Granny, I must agree with you on that. However, I say let her stay for one more month. It could be the fact that she knows there's no escape. I would hate for Mya to have to visit her at the graveyard.

"All right, son, if you say so." She was filled with great sadness. The only reason she didn't make a big fuss was because she knew that Cam would hold true to his words.

"If she remains true, then I'll bring her back. I got to go, baby. Take care of my daughter." He planted a soft kiss on her forehead. "Mona will be with me for a couple of days, so don't wait up for her."

Cam yelled up the steps, summoning me downstairs. I walked slowly and enticingly down the staircase. He marveled at my natural beauty. Even wearing a jean outfit, I was fine as ever. My blue rhinestone thong exposed just enough for others to take a second look. The sky blue halter-top I wore was trimmed in rhinestone and cut very low. There were rhinestones on the crease of my stilettos as well.

"What did you pack an overnight bag for?" he asked.

"Come on, now, baby, I know you—a day's outing can turn into several days or weeks. I'm prepared just in case it does. Have you decided on where we are going first?" I asked.

"Yeah, let's take a ride to see Prince." I almost choked on my spit. *Oh God, oh God, please tell me he doesn't know!* I prayed to myself, keeping my cool. Camron waited for my response, and not seeing much of one, he appeared pleased.

We pulled up to the borough and parked in front of the building. Niggas were all over. Camron opened the door for me and grabbed me close as we walked through the doors. I could care less about what happened in the past. Today he was treating me like a queen. Dudes looked on in desire while the women glared in shock. Nikki was the only chick he showed off in New York. It was my moment of fame in Brownsville. Camron was still that nigga.

Prince had no idea that Camron and I were paying him a visit. He was laid back in the living room, watching basketball when we arrived. "What up, Baby Pa?" Camron said.

"Nothing, B," Prince responded with the door halfway open.

"You gon' let us in or what!" Camron shouted.

"*Us,* who's *us?*" Prince asked, puzzled.

"Open the door and find out, nigga!"

Opening the door widely, Prince made eye-to-eye contact with me. "Speak to my bitch, nigga, don't just stare at her," Cam demanded.

Prince never spoke and just turned away. His woman, Dawn, appeared from the bedroom. "This is Dawn, my lady," Prince said in a monotone.

I was anxious to meet her. "Hi, Dawn, I'm Mona. I take it you heard about me."

"Yeah, I heard about you," she responded. "I bet it feels good to go other places besides the salon, doesn't it?" *What the fuck did she mean by that?* I let that comment slide because I was too busy studying the layout of the apartment. It was an average Brooklyn apartment—nothing special, and just like the apartment, Dawn was an average Brooklyn ho. *I wonder what Prince is doing with his money. This can't be his main crib or his main woman. Maybe he considers me his main woman.* I was thinking crazy.

"I thought we could all get together for the night. Controversy is throwing an album release party at that banging club on 137th Street in Manhattan," Cam said.

My eyes lit up. "Controversy, ooh, it's been a minute since I last seen him!" Prince watched my enthusiasm. I could tell he was catching true feelings for me. Dawn looked at me grudgingly. I figured she wasn't trying to spend the night with a star-struck Delaware groupie.

"I'll pass," Dawn said looking directly at Camron.

"Prince, get your bitch in order," Camron said. He waved his hand as if he was telling her to shut the fuck up.

"Bitch, who you calling a bitch!" she screamed. "I don't care how you treat your women, but you won't treat me like that."

"Whatever the fuck ever, bitch!" He didn't care whether or not Prince or Dawn was offended. Dawn was heated, not only by what Camron said, but also because of what went down with Nikki. Nikki was her best friend. I didn't give a care if she went with us or not because I would have both my men by my side. Then all the attention would be on the three of us. Anytime Cam or Prince made an appearance at a club, it was on! Tonight would definitely increase my chances with Controversy.

Prince looked at Dawn hesitantly before responding to Camron's request. "She's staying, so let's go." Dawn shook her head in amazement at how Prince didn't even bother to defend her.

"You and Mona can meet me in the car," Cam stated. "I have another stop to make." We proceeded without hesitation.

Prince thought that Cam was making a stop up the hall to see Cheryl, another one of his hoes. Cam convincingly walked toward the steps, and Prince and I got into the elevator. Then he strolled back to see Dawn. He was hot about Dawn not joining us. To him that was a form of disrespect. Knocking lightly, he entered the apartment and walked straight into the bedroom where Dawn was crying. Not bothering to turn around to see who it was, she began to talk.

"So, you decided not to go after all. How come you didn't stand up for me?" she asked.

"And why would I do that," Cam responded. Dawn jumped clear out the bed not knowing what to do. "I call them as I see them. A bitch is a bitch! Now come here, bitch!" Cam screamed.

"What is wrong with you?" she whimpered.

"You! What, you too good to hang out with a nigga like me, or are you just jealous of my chick? Which one?"

"Neither," she responded. "I just don't like you or your company."

"Is that right? I'll tell you what, then: We can have a party right here—you and me. Then we'll see how you enjoy my company." He grabbed her, forcing her to the floor. "Now, get on your knees!" He unzipped his pants and dared her to bite him. After he made her swallow every drop of his semen, he threatened her. "If you by chance mention this to your man, I will make sure to torture you every chance I get. And remember, no bitch is too good to be with me, willingly or unwillingly! You heard that...bitch!" he said very coldly.

Dawn had a helpless look on her face. She was humiliated but knew that he had meant what he said. Semen was dripping from her bottom lip.

I was all over Prince in the elevator. "What happened to you this week? You didn't stop and see me."

"I knew he was coming over, that's why," Prince said. "Figured he would hit you off this week. It would be best if we slowed down anyway. You're getting too comfortable with me. It's making me uneasy."

"Why shouldn't I? I have love for you." I planted a soft kiss on his lips.

"Time to go—off the elevator— now!" He shoved me off the elevator when the doors opened.

We walked to the car and he opened the passenger door for me. He sat in the car patiently without saying a word. Prince didn't like the idea of riding with us but went along with the boss's request. He could've simply driven his cream-colored Cadillac Escalade. I started in on him again.

"When you gon' let me ride in...I mean, get a ride in that pretty cream Escalade? Let's take a trip. Consider it, just you and I on an overnight trip, away from Granny and Cam. I wasn't really feeling your chick...so I finally got a chance to meet your lady. She's not what I expected—not that tall, a little on the chunky side, pale skin...hmmm...you can do better than that."

"How, by making you my woman?" he bellowed. "Damn, all you tricks are the same—always hating on the next chick!" Anyway, she's just one of my many women," he added, looking directly into my eyes. "And I don't have time to break off an overnight trip with you. Our Friday schedule is right in line with everything else, so don't try to change up now."

"You know you want to make love to me all damn day, not just a few hours here and there, so please stop fronting. Well, it's just too bad for Dawn that she didn't come along. We could've talked all night long. You know, bonded, or something like that. I probably would have learned a little bit about how she pleases you. And stop lying, Prince, you don't have enough time in a day...*many women.* I know your hectic schedule." He shifted in his seat, cringing at my every word. He was on edge.

"Mona, I don't know what you're trying to pull, but you might want to calm the fuck down. If Cam has a clue that we boning, both of us gon' end up missing. For the sake of our lives, be cool, okay?" Prince's nervousness was beginning to show. This was unlike him. Feeling self-assured, I handled him with ease.

"I'm cool, stop tripping. I like the sound of *we*— sounds more like we're a couple." Just as I finished the last word, Camron opened the car door on the driver's-side of the shiny black Benz 500 SL.

"Y'all ready to be out?"

We sure were, but not with him. A little solo time together was all that Prince and I needed.

Chapter 10

It's On & Poppin'

The club was packed wall to wall with major figures. Of course I was in heaven. All these men and me, oh my! I paid no mind to all the other beautiful women. My only concern was whose attention I could catch. We settled up in the V.I.P. section reserved by Controversy. I knew this was my chance to really meet him. *If only Nee was here to see this*, I thought.

"Excuse me, fellas, if you don't mind, I need to go freshen up." Cam and Prince both looked at me, knowing I was hot in the pants.

"I'm timing your ass, so make it quick," said Camron.

"I will, daddy." Moving swiftly, I sprinted out of the V.I.P. area. After studying Nikki's catwalk, I had mastered it perfectly. The focus was on me, as usual, and I bathed in all the lustful stares. In the bathroom the ladies were applying make-up and making comments. One of them made a comment about trying to get at Cam. That was cool, because if he remained preoccupied, I could make moves. I heard them while I was in the stall.

"Girl, did you see Cam up in this piece? I'm ready to jump all over his ass. He's still balling. Did you see that damn six-carat pinky ring he got on?"

The second girl responded. "No, girl, did you see that shit his girl got on?"

"I didn't see Nikki here."

"Nikki, that trick is old news. Her ass is all up in Kiesha's whorehouse. I'm talking about his new trick. That bitch is sharp as hell. Now, if you think you have a chance with her here, then by all means, do you!"

"Fo' sure! I don't care if she's here or not. Cam is a straight up trick and you know it. He might not disrespect her in front of us, but let me get him alone for a few minutes. I'll be able to set up my date. That's all I want from him—a date. She can have all the other drama. He won't try to kill *my* ass. I'll leave that for his baby mama and his whores. They gave each other high fives. I let them leave the bathroom before I exited, since I wanted miss thing's plan to go through. I would give her a few minutes to put her thing down while I was undercover.

On my way back to the table, I noticed the same females that were in the bathroom seated with both of my men. I was like, "Oh, hell no! I won't be disrespected like that." It was cool that the one chick wanted to holla at Cam, but I wasn't having the other chick holla at Prince. I wasn't willing to give them both up for the night. My adrenaline began to flow. Stepping up to the table, I gave both of them a serious look. They let me have my way, not wanting me to turn it out. My frown was quickly removed when I heard the voice of Controversy. I was ready for him this time. I turned around quickly so I could see him in full view. He wore a black Armani suit with a Gucci belt and 'gator shoes. His teeth were gleaming white, showing every time he smiled. I scanned his whole body. The bulge in his pants was calling my name! "What's up, Controversy? Mona's the name. I'm quite sure you remember me." My Angel fragrance lingered in the air as my body temperature started to rise.

"And how could I forget a beauty like you? You my man's lady, right?" he asked with an uncertain look on his face.

"Hell yeah!" Cam interjected. "Mona, sit your hot ass down and stop being so eager to be up in another dude's face," he added.

I wanted to yell out, "I don't have to be all up in his face, 'cause on the real, he eyeing me down." Still trying to feed his ego, I did as I was told, but only after bending to get my glass. I bent ever so gently, just to get my crystal blue rhinestone thong to show.

"Ouch! Damn, Mona, it's like that?" Controversy allowed the words to escape from his mouth. I knew that it was only a matter of time now.

"Yo, don't take it personal, my woman loves attention," Cam stated. Prince was boiling. He knew I wanted Controversy to hit me off. He didn't like it one bit. I was trying to play them all. Whispering in my ear, Prince told me to chill out. Remembering how he had spoken to me earlier, I totally ignored him. This was right up my alley. Before the night was up, Controversy slipped me his number.

Chapter 11

The Meeting

After two months, Yatta finally caught up with Darryl, before finding out that he had gotten jammed up. Just freshly out of turnkey, Darryl went to see Yatta.

"Where the hell have you been and where is my money, nigga?"

"Hold tight, I just got out of turnkey. I got popped dropping off over Southbridge to Kenny and them. Didn't they tell you?"

"No, man, you should have written a kite." Yatta wasn't trying to hear that weak excuse.

"Man, I was too busy working on my biceps for the ladies."

Yatta shook his head at Darryl's dumb ass. "How did you get popped?"

"Speeding past the police station, that's how," replied Darryl.

"You know that shit gon' cost you. My New York connection was on my ass. I'm following up on your story, and if it's incorrect, expect to be in a body bag. Make sure you bring me double what you owe me too, son. You're dismissed."

"No doubt," Darryl replied. He didn't make a fuss about bringing back double 'cause he knew he messed up.

Yatta decided to contact Nieka to find out if she had heard from me. "Nee, what's up, baby?" Have you talked to my sister, yo?"

"Boy, please, ever since she hooked up with Camron she barely calls and never visits. She don't even mess with Won Sumth'n Clique. Now you know she's gone, the way they hung out every day."

"Well, I'm taking a trip up top today. You wanna ride out with me?"

"I don't know." She was very hesitant. "I'd have to pay a babysitter and all."

"Stop acting like a punk bitch!" Yatta screamed. "I'll give you more than enough money for a babysitter. Now get dressed and wear something nice...meaning no sneakers, all right?"

He knew he had to guide her on the dress code. After talking to her, he called Cam to inform him of his anticipated arrival time. Things were back to normal since he had paid off his debt.

When they arrived in New York the weather was grim. Gray skies and thunderstorms filled the atmosphere with gloom. Cam arranged for them to meet at Kiesha's spot. Looking around the apartment building, Nee was getting rather nervous. Yatta was relaxed and suggested that she do the same, but Nee was filled with fear.

"I don't know what you got me into, but I don't like it. It seems rather creepy here. Look at all these people staring at us like they ready to rob us or something, and plus it's cold and rainy."

"Would you chill the fuck out? Damn, you talk too much! Just get on the elevator and push the twelfth floor," Yatta said. Actually, he wanted her along for the company and to carry his pack. The duffel bag was secured tightly around his shoulders, holding $120,000 of re-up money.

People were lined up against the wall trying to get into Kiesha's. "What the hell is going on here?" Nee thought. They went straight to the door and requested to see Cam.

"Nigga, who you?" Kiesha asked. Being far from pretty, she was charcoal black, had two missing teeth, nappy hair and a foul smell.

"Damn! The question is, who the hell is your ugly ass?" Yatta replied. This was his first time meeting Cam at Kiesha's.

"Oh, you must be that kid from Delaware Cam told me was coming. Come on in. What you bring the chick for, she turning tricks or something?"

"Hell no, I'm not turning no tricks," Nee said defensively.

"Don't be offended, miss thang, that's what women usually come in here for. I was just trying to figure out what my cut would be. Let me page the boss to let him know you're here."

Kiesha and Cam were from the same neighborhood. He saw Kiesha at her best before getting cracked out. She was one of the few women Cam trusted. That's only because she allowed him to use her house for his tricks.

Yatta and Nee observed men coming in, one by one, and leaving very pleased. "Excuse me, Kiesha, but how many women do you have tricking in your house?" Nee asked.

"Look-a-here...a concerned trick. You feel the need to help out?" said Kiesha.

"No, I'm just saying, it's like forty dudes lined up outside. I know one woman can't handle all these men."

"If you need to know, there are four of them. They do women as well, so if you're up to it, I'll let you skip the line!"

Yatta was in tears of laughter. "That's what the hell she gets for being so damn nosey."

Nee sat down and didn't say another word. She began to feel very uncomfortable. "I've never been in a situation like this. Why did you bring me here?" she whispered to Yatta.

"Just relax, sweetheart, it'll be okay," he said smiling. "Right now, I want to see who the stars are. Who y'all got—Del Rio or 'Pagne up in this mother?"

"Nigga, peep shows cost ten bucks, so if you're a spectator and want to watch, all three will be thirty," Kiesha hollered out.

Yatta handed her thirty dollars and watched her place the money inside her saggy bra. Walking back toward the rooms, he said to Kiesha, "You may wanna put a little something extra in that bra, or your money might fall out."

"So, I guess we have a comedian in the house...real funny, like Chris Rock," she replied.

The air was filled with sex and the smell of crack. It didn't bother Yatta one bit. This was something he was used to. Opening the peep slot to the first bedroom, he watched a badass Hispanic chick with bouncing breasts doing two dudes at once. When she noticed she had a spectator, she made sure it was worth watching. She allowed one guy to enter her from behind while the other straddled her in the front. They looked like a chocolate oreo cookie all smashed together. The men were in heaven.

In the middle bedroom a dude was receiving oral sex from a chick that was butt-ass naked, wearing thigh-high, patent leather boots. It seemed like the norm until the trick lifted her head. She was a transvestite. "What da hell is goin' on in here?" said Yatta.

In the last room he watched two women and one man. Both of the women were beautiful, wearing sexy dominatrix outfits, exposing their breasts and the fatness of their pearls. While the man positioned one of the women doggy-style, the other one spanked him with a long, horse-tailed leather whip. "Now that's what I'm talkin' 'bout!" Yatta screamed. "What more could a man ask for than to hit two nasty hookers!" He never heard Cam come in.

"Listen at his stupid ass," Cam laughed. "Fool, let's get down to business. What you bring the broke ho along for?"

"She's my sister's best friend. You know her, right?" asked Yatta.

"I know who she is. My brother hit her the first night they met."

"Word, son? So did I," said Yatta. They both laughed. "She's carrying my pack back after she sees Mona. Where is Mona, anyway?" Yatta asked with concern.

"She's safe," Cam replied. "I'll have her meet us in front of the building around six o'clock."

Chapter 12

It's Over Now

I was back at Granny's feeling like my old self. The stereo system was blaring. My spirit was running free. I danced all over the room, looking at myself in the three-fold mirror on the dresser. My body swayed vivaciously to the sounds of Controversy. Just as I thought, Camron decided to drop me off so he could be with the chick from the club. I didn't even care. He was so predictable! That's one of the reasons I started to sleep with Prince. He thought he was getting over on me, but I was getting over on him. Really, we were playing one another! You have to admit, though, I was better at it than he was. I had no doubt about that.

I continued to sway, allowing my body to flow freely as I began feeling Controversy more and more. Thinking I had rap skills, I grabbed my brush and spit my own rhyme to the mesmerizing beat.

See I'm that B-I-T-C-H you want to fuck withCan't none y'all sluts touch thisDon't let the fat ass and brown eyesfool you niggaI'll put a nine to your headbefore I hit that triggerLeave your family in mourning,hit that safe clean it outbefore I bone your main manleave his ass in a state of confu-shan Jet out on a plane to Tahiti,sunbathe all alone on the beach,plotting on that next sweetie

"Damn, I'm tight! That's what I'm talkin' 'bout. I need to be on *Freestyle Fridays* or *Making the Cut*, for real. Free, Ajay, holla at your girl!"

Walking through the door, Prince shook his head. "You'll never change. That's all you think about, getting money from a man. What's up with that? What happened to you going to college? You still have plenty of time, you know. You're an intelligent young woman, Mona."

"Look!" I responded. "Don't be coming around here talking that righteous shit. I'm not trying to hear that. I don't need college. I have all I need right here; so please, save all the drama, mister man. Anyway, how you gon' try to front on me when your woman don't even have a high school diploma? Why are you so concerned about me going to college? You gon' pay my way to attend?"

Prince was getting tired of my mouth. "So, what, you think you're a rapper now?" he laughed. "Who told you you could rhyme—Controversy? The way he was up on you last night I'm surprised he didn't get at you."

"And what is it to you if he did?" I asked cunningly. You must remember; I'm only a hit-and-miss for you. When we started in this relationship, I told you I needed a *little* love, not a lot. You served the purpose at the time."

"That nigga did try to holla, didn't he? You were game, too...I bet your sneaky ass was! Damn, you greasy, Mona. Cam has no idea what kind of chick you are."

"Are you going to tell him? Of course not, 'cause if you do, you know what he'll do to you. I didn't put a gun to your head. You were ready and willing to hit this. It's apparent that you're not loyal to him either."

Prince had had enough of me. He wanted to end what should've never begun. "Let me get out this piece before I kill your ass! The next time you see me, don't even acknowledge I'm in the same room.

You put a nasty taste in my mouth. One day this shit is gon' come back on you, Mona."

"Well, maybe it already has. Growing up my life was hell. It's my time to reap the benefits. See ya, Prince; it's been real! I still got love for you, though!" I wasn't mad just because he was. I murmured to him as he walked out the door. "Move over, it's his turn now, move over, it's his turn now, your game got shut down... sorry!"

Dear Journal:

Shit is getting a little crazy! I don't think Prince wants to fool around with me anymore. I don't give two flying fucks! That nigga is history...done with! Ya' heard me? I had Controversy's attention at the club. It was only a matter of time. I thought I told you! I'm-a dig in his pants and dig in them good, when I get the chance. Cam's slick ass went out with that whore from the club. She got what she wanted. Damn, why can't I? I'm not asking for much. I know what, though, I'm getting tempted like hell with all the money in these rooms. It sure would be nice to secure my pension with that. I could go home and live lovely without side hustling. Granny is getting on my damn nerves. I don't like the way she looks at me. She probably jealous 'cause she don't have the shape I do. Yeah, I know she's old, but old women still think they cute. She shouldn't be such a damn hater! Tell me why I keep thinking about what's going on at home. Maybe later I'll call and get updated on the news. I'm quite sure it will take all of five minutes to get all the scoop from Nee. Till next time...Precioustymes!

Chapter 13

Change Is Good

Since Prince wasn't going to be popping in anymore, I had time to find out more information about Ms. Nikki. Even with Granny downstairs in the kitchen fixing breakfast I was able to snoop. She would be down there at least till noon, when she was ready to lay Mya down for a nap.

My footsteps were heavy, walking through the hallway as if it was okay to roam through Granny's belongings. I must be slipping. I should've had this information a month ago. Instead, what did I do, get caught up with another dude. *Stay on top of your game, bitch. Stop slipping, a dude gon' be around regardless.* I had to motivate myself.

I opened the chest holding the birth certificate documents. Let me pull all this shit out. I know there's more to this story. Setting aside two bundles of money, I examined a yellow manila folder. Look what I've found. A death certificate with the name Drew Moore. Wait a minute, here's a birth record and a death record! I read the coroner's comments.

Januuary 30, 2002: The cause of death for a black male, birth name, Drew Moore, is heart failure and kidney failure due to multiple shots to the head, heart, abdomen and groin area.

What the hell? Looking further I found the police report. *Oh shit! What have I gotten myself into?* The police report acknowledged Alexander King as the number one suspect for Drew's murder. I read the police report out loud:*January 25, 2002: Nikki Moore, wife of Drew Moore, called to report a dispute between victim, Drew Moore, and suspect, Alexander King. Allegedly, the caller intervened when the suspect forced the victim, Drew Moore, at gunpoint into a black 2002 LS 400 Lexus Coupe. As reported by caller, her husband never returned—only the suspect the following day. Officer Hairston took a Missing Persons report and a warrant issued for the arrest of Alexander King. Construction workers uncovered the body of an unidentified black male, later identified as one Drew*

Moore, found under the Verrazano Bridge. The victim was shot fourteen times with a Mac-10. Suspect, Alexander King, was held twenty-four hours for questioning, but ordered released due to lack of evidence.

I covered my left eye and sighed. An instant headache filled my head.

*Her husband...*the trick was married. I guess she wasn't lying about Cam's real name.

Who is Nancy Johnson, I thought. I wondered if Drew was Mya's father. I knew what I needed to do—call Prince, he'd know the answers. But after the way I had treated him earlier, I figured he might not tell me. I couldn't call him on the phone. I decided to pay him a visit.

Placing the documents back into the chest, I gave into temptation and grabbed the two bundles of money, roughly amounting to $500,000 a bundle. Keeping up with the allowance money Cam sent regularly, it gave me a chance to stack my paper. My allowance combined with the $1,000,000 came to $1,250,000—money I never experienced in my life. This would be more than enough to get me on my feet.

I ran quickly back into my bedroom to grab both my oversized Louis Vuitton duffel bags. Hopefully, they would hold all the money. Running back to the room as fast as I could, I grabbed the bundles of money, stuffing them into the bags tightly. I could feel this lifestyle coming to an end.

Out of nowhere, I began to feel guilty about not contacting my family or friends since getting with Cam. I thought about my mom and wondered how she was making out, or whether or not she decided to change her life around. I wondered what Grandma was doing. Yatta, I knew, was all right. I was sure of that 'cause he had always been a soldier. I had to bring myself back. It was no time to think of them. I had business to take care of. My thoughts just wouldn't go away, so I decided to call home later.

Putting everything back into place, I eased out of the bedroom and headed down the hall with my bags. I placed them in the linen closet, which was rarely used. Now, I had to figure out how I was going to get them to the car without Granny seeing me.

Granny never turned down the money Camron sent her, but I would often hear her praying all the time about the "blood money." The only time she went in the rooms was to put money away. I figured since the money bundles were on the bottom it would be a long time before she knew that any money was missing—that's if she ever realized the money was gone.

Sitting in my Jeep, I contemplated on how I was going to get the bags of money out of the house. That's when I noticed Granny frantically waving at me. "What the hell does she want?" I thought. Making an effort to not be disrespectful, I turned off the car and walked up the driveway. "Yes, Ma'am?" Granny didn't crack a smile or move her lips to speak. She handed me the phone and walked away. "Hello?" I said.

"Where the hell are you going?" It was Cam.

"Um, I'm headed out to get some females things, you know, that time is coming."

"You lying ass!" he replied.

"I'm not lying, I'm serious," I said, trying to convince him.

He interrupted me before I could say more. "I need you to meet me in front of Kiesha's building at six."

"Why?" I said stuttering. "Wha...what's up?" I asked slowly.

"Just be here at six o'clock, that what's up, and don't be late. One!"

Damn! That messed up my plans. "What's he up to?" I thought. Before anything ungovernable jumped off, I decided to call my mother to see how the family was doing. The phone rang several times before someone answered. Just when I decided to hang up I heard a voice on the receiving end.

"Praise the Lord!"

"*Praise the Lord!* I must have the wrong number! I'm sorry, I'm trying to reach the Foster residence."

"Mona, baby, is that you?"

"Mom, is that you?" I was baffled.

"Oh, baby, I have been praying that you would finally call. I've been so worried about you. Where are you? Where you living? Who you with? Why haven't you called? We've all been so worried about you!"

"Mom, Mom...slow down. First off, did I hear you say, 'Praise the lord?' Since when you start talking about God?"

"Oh, baby, since you've been gone I've turned my life over to the Lord. I'm saved, delivered, sanctified and filled with the Holy Ghost! Hallelujah! He has removed the blindfolds from my eyes and now I can see. Thank you Jesus!"

I went into a brief state of shock as my mother continued to give praise to the Lord. My mom was in church. "What? Mom, I've never heard you talk about God. What's this all about?"

"See, baby, the Lord moves in mysterious ways. When God calls you, you must submit or deal with His wrath. Whether you're ready or not, it's on His time. I know I haven't been the best role model or parent that I should have been. I know I've put men, drugs and alcohol before my children. I'm deeply hurt, because I know that hurt my children. But I give honor to God that he was able and willing to receive me even in the midst of my mess. I vowed to God that if he delivered me and bestowed mercy and grace upon my soul, I would live the rest of my days praising and worshipping him. Hallelujah! Thank you, Jesus. I've been on my knees praying that you would call. And oh, how God answers prayers! You must believe in him, Mona, lest your spirit will die."

"Mom, please! I didn't call for this. I'm happy you found God and all but after all these years, please don't try to preach to me about doing *God's will.*"

"God told me your heart would be hardened, but I won't give up! If I have to pray forty days and forty nights, like Noah, I will! Praises to God!"

"Before you continue on, Mom, I called to tell you I'm sending you a care package. You should get it by the end of the week. Look for two large boxes. UPS will deliver them. Oh yeah, I'm fine and living gracefully. Tell Grandma I love her."

"Mona, please don't go. Let me pray for you before you hang up. Prayer changes things! This is your chance to give your heart to the Lord."

"No, Mom, I think I've had enough church for the day—talk with you soon—love you!"

"I love you more, baby. May God have mercy upon your soul."

I couldn't believe my Mom got saved. Man, what was the world coming to? My headache intensified. Why now? What stunt was she trying to pull? This was a first for me. *God...God?* I couldn't let it daunt me. I had work to do. I walked into the house.

Granny was sitting in the kitchen dozing off. I took advantage of it and ran upstairs to get the duffel bags. After I placed each one in the back seat, I felt dazed and confused. Granny suddenly appeared in the doorway. She was probably watching me and listening the whole time I was at the Jeep. Not knowing what to say or do, I handed her the phone. Granny didn't respond with her usual sarcasm but told me to take heed to what my mother had said. Yeah, she was listening.

"Granny, no disrespect, but you was ear hustling. That conversation was between me and my mother."

"See, that's where you're wrong, young lady. When it comes to God, all spiritual mothers are involved," she responded sharply.

"How can you sit there and try to reprimand me like you don't know what's really happening in your house? Stop acting like you're blind! And how can you sit there and act like nothing is going on with Nikki and Cam?"

"My faith, although only the size of a small mustard seed, is what keeps me going. You wouldn't understand that because you're worldly. You are the one who's blind. I know that God's going to work it out! Now get going, young lady before I lay hands on you! The devil is a liar and there is no truth in him!"

"Granny, you can try to use the Lord as your crutch, but I know for sure he's not pleased with your involvement. You are conspiring with a drug dealer. Why? Why are you doing it? Ask yourself that! Is it for the sake of Mya...Nikki, or is it because you benefit from all of this? Your social security check alone can't pay the mortgage on this extravagant house. I'm not trying to disrespect you, but you need to stop fronting like you don't know what's up!" This was all too much for me—first my mom and now Granny. "What is this, some kind of God conspiracy?" I thought to myself.

"Let me get out of here," she said, trying to avoid eye contact with me. She never questioned me about the duffel bags, and boy, was I happy. I prayed that she wouldn't tell Cam about our little fellowship conversation.

Dear Journal:

I'm in trouble now. I let Granny's old ass have it. I don't care if Cam finds out or not. She needs to stop acting like she's so innocent—going to church on Sunday and right back sinning on Monday. She know damn well what Cam and Prince are about. And Cam told her about Nikki tricking, so that would mean she's okay with prostitution, too, right? Oh, but I'm the sinner in the house. Somebody needs to check that. Then to top that off, stuff is really strange. People ain't who they say they are. All these names keep popping up on documents. One good thing—I got the money! That's all I'm really concerned about, and getting it back home. I'm out. Till next time...Precioustymes!

Blessed is he whose transgression is forgiven, whose sin is covered.

Psalm:32:1-KJV

Chapter 14

Controversy

Driving so fast down Fulton Street, I almost missed my turn. There were a few hours to play before meeting up with Cam. I was debating on whether or not to see Prince first or to stop by Controversy's crib. If I stopped at Controversy's, I knew I'd get hit off. That would take an hour or so. If I stopped at Prince's, it would take about an hour to pull the information from him. That would be two hours between the two of them. And I'd already spent a half hour at the UPS office.

I pulled up to the brownstone building and examined the area closely before deciding to park three blocks away. Just in case Cam decided to come around, this would throw him off. While quickly freshening my face, I noticed my journal, peeking through the edge of the back seat. Damn, I had forgotten to include it in the package.

After putting my journal inside my Coach bag, I paid Controversy a visit. I didn't think twice about knocking. Looking out his peephole, Controversy wasn't the least bit surprised. He knew I would follow up after last night in the club.

"Miss Mona, what a delight to see you! What brings you here?" he asked with a sly grin.

"Are you kidding me? I've been waiting for this day!" I responded. "Are you home alone?"

"Not anymore." He gestured for me to enter. "Please do come in," he said. It was clear that this was a bachelor's pad. The view was nice but not quite like Granny's.

"What's that smell?" I asked.

"It's lavender aromatherapy. It soothes the soul. Did you know that, Miss, Mona?

"Of course, I know that." I didn't have a clue what lavender was, let alone aromatherapy. I was bullshittin' him.

Controversy was seven years older than I was and much more mature. "Can I get you something to drink—a glass of wine, hypnotiq... anything?" he asked.

"I'll take a glass of hypnotiq. That sounds exotic," I said, smiling.

"Have a seat in the lounge. I'll be right back," he said, walking toward the kitchen area. Sitting there in amazement, I realized that I was living out one of my fantasies. I watched as his large chocolate arms swayed from side to side. His demeanor was thuggish. Even his tattoos pulsated with his stride. It was obvious that he was well hung from the thickness of his inner thighs. He was a black beauty. I was going to let him have his way with me.

Nestling myself in the oversized lounge chair, I made myself at home. "I haven't watched television in so long," I said, glancing at his flat screen t.v.

"Well, that's good, 'cause I was thinking we could make our own movie. Are you down for that?" he asked with a devious grin.

"What the hell are you talking about, Controversy?"

"You know, an adult movie."

"A movie...I've never been taped before. I don't know if I'm with that," I responded.

"You mean to tell me you're not in any of Cam's movies?"

"What movies? Cam doesn't make any movies...or does he? He's into a lot of things I don't know about."

"That's what I've been trying to tell you all along!" Controversy used my lust for him to his advantage. He badmouthed Cam, hating on every facet of his world. "Ma, Cam is the underground king of porno. He has over three hundred movies 'round the city."

"Stop playing, Controversy."

"The only reason I let him swing with me was because of the money he was bringing the crew from his movies. On tour there's always groupies hanging out waiting for an opportunity to get hit off...just like you."

"What did you say, Controversy? See, you're playing with me!"

"Why would I be playing with you? I have no reason to lie. It's true. Most of the women stick around trying to get the chance to sex one of the rappers, his boys, security guards or anybody they think can get them close to major figures. They're willing to screw themselves to the top; so we, in turn, use that as an opportunity to make money by exploiting them. That way, none of us will ever be charged with sexual assault. Everything's videotaped, which means we always have evidence."

"Now, you down for making a movie or what? This can be your debut."

"I'm sorry, sweetie, I can't be taped. If Cam got a hold of it, he would kill my ass."

"Cam doesn't give a damn about you, Mona! If he did, then why didn't he allow you on the road trips? Most of the crew brings their ladies along, even if they do stay in the hotel during the show. I bet he never asked you to come along, did he?"

"No, he didn't, because he feared that I would try to get with you."

"Guess he was right, 'cause you're here now and not just for conversation, so let's make a movie...come on, now, ma...it would be solely for me. I've been wanting you all this time. We've longed for each other. Now, honestly, you know we have a better chance in hell trying to get ice water than to be in a relationship. I wouldn't even play myself like that, but since we have the chance we can make a movie, and when you're gone I can rewind the tape over and over to remind me of the wonderful time we shared." He spoke slowly and carefully as he kissed my neck. He was so convincing and I tried hard to resist, but he looked too damn fine to pass up—even if he was playing me.

Finally, I submitted to his request. "As long you promise not to let anybody watch it."

He started pulling my shirt over my head as he continued to kiss my neck. "Oh, baby, you know this will be only for me!"

Like a disorderly animal, I ripped off his white wife beater to caress his tight muscular chest. I licked his nipples, driving him wild. My hands roamed all over his body, allowing loose-fitting jeans to fall to his ankles. *Oh my God, he's got the magic stick!* It popped up as soon as his boxers came down. Looking at it, I wasn't sure if I could measure up to his standards. I tried to calculate the measurements in my mind...ten to twelve inches long and about three to four inches thick. Could I work with that? I was definitely going to try.

I whispered in his ear as he fought to loosen my bra. "Controversy, I want you to know the only reason I hooked up with Cam was to get close to you. Please, don't treat me like a groupie. I wanted you from the start, but Cam kind of took control of me. The money started to fill my thoughts, but my mind stayed on you. I was so happy to see you at the club that I almost followed you home; however, you and Camron left with those two groupies. I was mad as hell at you."

After finally getting my bra loose, he gripped my shoulders tightly before grabbing my head and sticking his long thick tongue into my mouth. I sucked on his tongue hungrily, enjoying the taste of his juices. Our kiss was so wet that saliva dripped as we pulled back for air. I wanted his scent all over my body, to smell it, drink it, whatever way I could have it. He moaned out my name, "Mona." His voice made me quiver on the inside. This was really happening. I was finally going to feel Controversy's magic stick inside me. I was butt- ass naked with the exception of my stiletto boots. Using his muscular abilities, he picked me up and forced his penis into my wet opening. I liked to die! I moaned and moaned as each stroke entered deeper and deeper inside of me. Tilting my head back, I could see the camcorder's red button flashing. We were being taped. It was too late to stop; I had already entered sexual bliss. My head wobbled with every thrust. He fell back on the sofa and grabbed my breasts as I clutched his head with my hands and rode him to no end. He then lifted my body and I held him tightly, kissing his earlobes. He carried me to his bedroom and laid me softly on the bed. In a whisper he said, "I'll be right back."

I soon learned that cameras were even in the bedroom. By the time Controversy pressed record, it was too late to say anything. This one was on the house.

Chapter 15

The Reunion

Cam impatiently paced in front of the project building. Nee was scared shitless while Yatta maintained his composure. "Where the hell is she? I told her to meet us here at six o'clock. It's now three minutes after six and she's still not here."

"Man, maybe she got caught in traffic. She'll be here." Yatta knew his sister. She was always late.

"Look at her dumb ass," said Cam, pointing to Nee. "You trust her scared ass to take back a pack? That's what's wrong with you Delaware hustlers. Y'all trust these hookers way too much. Man, you have to watch them closer than you watch your own crew.

Y'all will learn," he said as he watched all the cars go by. "Here she comes now!"

I was in the car trying to fix my hair and put my face back on. I knew Cam would be pissed about me being late; so I had to come up with an excuse. I double-parked and jumped out. *Damn! That looks like Nee. Oh shit, it is Nee!*

Noticing me, Nee ran over to me like she hadn't seen me in years. "Hey whore! How you been? Why haven't you called?"

"I'm fine, ho. How'd you get up here?"

"Yatta had to take care of some business. I came along for the ride."

"Unh-uh, knowing my brother, you came for business, too. Weren't you the same one who told me that bringing packs back are for the birds? Oh, no, the exact words were, 'You still into that shit!' "

"Mona, everybody doesn't have it like you. I've been busting my ass trying to make it for my daughter and me. Sometimes a little extra cash can help out. Anyway, you look good, girl! Cam must be taking good care of you! Well, you know your mom got saved. It's all over town. Nobody would've ever thought your crazy-ass mom would give her heart to the Lord."

"Believe it or not, I talked to her earlier and she told me. That's all good, but right now, I have to deal with the devil. Oh, and remind me to tell you whose house I just came from." I was blushing from ear to ear.

"Whoever it was did a job on your neck!"

"What?" I replied. I hadn't realized there were bright red marks around my neck. "Damn! I'm getting careless big time. That's from the hot wax Controversy put on me. Is it very visible?"

"Those spots are red as candy apples, girl! Hold up, whore! Did you say Controversy? What you gon' do? That man you got is a stone fool."

"Girl, who you telling, I know. Stay by my side and don't leave until I give you the cue." I had to put my adventure with Controversy on hold for the time being. I was still riding high off the energy, but my ass was sore and I couldn't move as fast as I normally could.

Nee looked at me attentively. "I'd like to see your slick ass get out of this one! If he pulls out his gat, I'm ducking!" As we walked toward Cam and Yatta, I began to put on a serious front. If he had any idea that I had been with another man, I would be history.

"Hey, daddy! I had a ball last night."

"I bet you did, hot ass. My thought was to smash your head in, but instead I let you shine 'cause you hadn't been out in a while. Now, show your man some love." He reached over to hug and kiss me. When he pulled back, I began to feel my gut rumble. He was still fine as ever, I couldn't deny that. Even though I enjoyed my time with Controversy, I started to question myself on what man I was truly in love or lust with. They all had unique qualities about them. If I could just take a little bit from this one and a little bit from that one, I could make a sure 'nough man. *Could I ever date just one man without all the high expectations?*

"Where the hell you been?"

"I was trying to get some cortisone cream to ease the pain from the hives on my neck." I showed him the redness on my neck.

"Damn, what happened to you?"

"I think it was something I ate. You know I'm allergic to peaches. Something I ate must have had some peaches or peach juice in it. I don't know, but it sure does itch." I started to scratch intensely. Yatta looked at me and shook his head. He could tell when I was lying. Giving Nee the cue, I proceeded as if nothing ever happened. "Hey, big bro. Give your little sister some love." Yatta embraced me and whispered in my ear to stop playing games with Cam.

"How long y'all gon' be up here?" I asked, trying to prolong their stay.

Cam cut in. "They only stayed a minute to see you. And a minute has passed."

"Oh, that's why you wanted to meet me at six. You should've told me to come sooner. We could've had lunch or something."

"Lunch, what they need lunch for when they're on business? And, really, it's time for them to go. It's getting hot around here." Cam demanded they leave for Delaware before the po-po decided to make their rounds.

"I understand, daddy, just give me a few more minutes with Nee, please." Nee and I walked toward the Jeep, and I began to talk freely. I was dying to tell her the details. "Girl, yes, I just left from Controversy's house. Can you believe it?"

"You are lying!" She showed doubt, but I wasn't mad, though.

"No, I'm not. I have a tape to prove it." I danced in circles as I watched her response.

"A tape?" She looked at me as if I was out of my mind.

"You know, videotapes, as in a movie."

"You let him record you!" I could tell she didn't approve, but who the hell cared. I had the one-on-

one spotlight with Controversy; I didn't have to share him at all.

"Why not? It was amazing too, girl, he got that *magic stick*. I have the tape under the driver's seat of my Jeep. I can't wait to watch it!"

"Is that the only tape?" she asked.

"No, he made two—one for me and one for him."

"Why would you do something that dumb? Mona, even I know better than to be taped. You let a rap star film you on tape? He's not even your man. I could see if it was your man, but a rapper? You know how many women he probably did that to! You acting just like one of those groupie chicks. I bet he didn't treat you any different than he would've if he'd picked you up from a concert."

"Look, Nee, just get in my Jeep and act like you're fascinated by the interior, grab the tape, put it in your purse and take it home. I don't care nothin' 'bout what you just said. I wasn't at a concert. I was in the privacy of his home. How many chicks get a chance to go to his resting place? I did. Just make sure you watch it, too. Girl, I worked him over real well! I am sore as hell from that magic stick of his. He's got an extra big one, fo' sure!"

"You are such a slut. Was he worth it, trick? Did you say he was packing? Did he give it to you right?" We both laughed.

"I told you, he was three loaves of bread, a pound of ham, turkey, American cheese and some honey mustard to go with it. I didn't want to leave, and he didn't want me to leave either. Had it not been for that crazy man, I'd be spending the night." I could see the envy beginning to show on Nee's face. Nee was jealous in her own way. She resented my driven spirit. She knew that once I set my mind to something, I would follow through to the end.

Our laughter ended with the sound of Cam calling me.

"Well, girl, you know what that means. It was so good seeing you."

"Mona, when you coming home? I'm afraid something bad is going to happen to you up here."

"No matter where I am, if something bad is going to happen, it will. I'll be home by the end of the week."

"For real...to stay?" She had the look of uncertainty in her eyes.

"Maybe for a few months, but I need to take care of some business before coming back."

"Is your man gon' let you come home?" The puzzled look on her face revealed that my words were unbelievable.

"He has no choice. I'm leaving him."

"What?" Are you crazy?"

I had to repeat myself for her to really take me seriously. "You heard me right. I've saved up enough money to live comfortably without a hustler. When I come home, I'll be on some other shit—maybe get enrolled at Springfield College, major in Human Services or Criminal Justice. My cousin is a good friend of the dean's. Remember, the reason we went to the concert was for me to get with Controversy. It took me some time, but I accomplished what I set out to do. I don't need to travel to other states to live in the limelight. New York has done enough of that for me. It's so fast here. I'd rather live in slow Delaware any day. Wilmington is calling my name!" We shared laughs again. "This life is taking its toll on my mind, body and spirit."

"Mona, if I didn't know any better, I'd think you're headed down the same path as your mother." Nee was getting a little sentimental.

"Well, not exactly. I'm not ready for the *God thing* yet. But I'm finally realizing I have deep issues in my life that I need to deal with. If anything happens to me before I come home, let my mother, grandmother and brother, know that I've always loved them. Also, I sent two UPS packages to my mother today. Follow up with her in a couple days to make sure she received them. Inside one of the packages is a journal." I had forgotten about not mailing the journal and not wanting Nee to know about the money. "If anything happens to me, all the information she needs is in there."

"Mona, please! You're making me cry. Why don't you leave with us now?"

"I can't, Nee. He won't let me. Have faith in me. Have I ever failed you? Don't I always come through?"

"Yeah, you always do." She knew that trying to convince me was a dead issue. "Okay, get going. I love you, girl!" I knew she had love for me like a blood sister.

"I love you too, Nee. You're my sister for life." We hugged and kissed before saying our farewells, and I walked over to my brother and embraced him once more. "Be safe and stay strong for your sister, bro. Take care of Mom and be sensitive to her needs during her walk with the Lord."

"So, you heard?" he said.

"Yeah, I heard, and I think it was time for her. Maybe it will be a trickle-down effect. The Lord can turn our lives around, too. Take care, bro...wait a minute. Did you go inside Kiesha's apartment?"

"Yeah, why?"

"Did you see a tall, light-skinned model-type chick turning tricks in there?"

"It was a couple of broads in that piece. Hold up, I do remember seeing two chicks who looked too good to be turning tricks. But in New York, looks don't mean shit. You know up here, everybody got a hustle."

"Thanks, bro."

Cam was busy talking with some dudes across the street from the building. He wasn't paying me any mind. I slipped inside the project building and headed to Kiesha's apartment. I had to see with my own eyes that Nikki was really turning tricks. The hallway lights were dim and the walls were filthy. It felt like I was crushing roaches with every step. A mouse, apparently not afraid of coming in contact with humans, slowly crept down the hall. *How do people live like this?*

This shit was giving me the creeps. I thought I had it bad back home, but this was poverty. I walked right into Kiesha's apartment as if I was a regular.

"Uh-uh! Who is this prissy bitch just walking up into my crib?" Kiesha said. "What is it you need, hun? I know you didn't come here for a hit. All the dealers are gone till eight o'clock."

I looked around, observing the filth, twitching my nose to the foul smell in the air. "I'm looking for Nikki."

"Nikki, who the hell is Nikki?"

"Cam's old girl. Isn't she here?"

"Ain't a trick in here by that name. And Cam would never send one of his women up in here. If you want to check, though, that will be thirty dollars—ten dollars to search each bedroom," she said, holding out her hand.

I handed her a fifty-dollar bill. "The extra is to keep your mouth shut about me being in here."

"I don't even know your name, sweetie."

"Good, keep it that way!" I walked quickly to the bedrooms. Upon opening the first door, I observed a young Hispanic chic. "Damn, girl! It smells like you need three or four douches up in that...a Norform or something! This room smells fishy as hell! You might want to pay a visit to the clinic, find out if you have bacteria vaginosis or something. Didn't your mama tell you that letting too many men run up in your coochie makes its smell? The sperm doesn't mix. Try using condoms. It may save your life, and if not that, it might spare the next person in the room from smelling your funky ass!"

I quickly closed the door and raised my head in disgust. When I peeked in the second room, I couldn't believe my eyes. Kenny, Cam's brother, was fucking a transvestite! He never came off as being gay or going both ways. These are things you never know, though, especially if it's a down low brotha! I bet Nee didn't know that. I pray to God that she made him wear a condom when he ran up in her.

The room was a filthy mess. It stank of ass and incense, and the smell didn't mix. Clothes were spread out all on the floor. There was only one dresser with two loose drawers. The transvestite wore a long-ass horse ponytail. It was hard for me to determine at first if it was truly a man or not, but when I saw the balls swinging back and forth, I knew for sure! Not even noticing that it was me, Kenny yelled, "Get the fuck out of here!" *Damn, I didn't know he went both ways; the things that go on behind closed doors.* I knew I had to hurry before he was finished.

There was only one woman in the last room. From behind she looked like Nikki, but when she turned around her face told a different story. "Nikki? Oh, my goodness, look at you!" For the first time, I felt really sorry for her.

"What are you doing here, Mona?" she said very sourly. "Why don't you go before Cam finds out you're here?"

"Nikki, please answer a few questions for me."

"What do you need to know now?" She lit a cigarette and took a long pull.

"Since when did you start smoking cigarettes?" I asked.

"I've *been* a smoker, just not around Cam. He hates for females to smoke."

"Can I ask you a question, and you give me an honest answer?"

"I won't make any promises, but I'll do my best."

"Who is Drew Moore?"

Nikki rose from the bed. "How did you find out about him?" she snapped.

"Please, just tell me."

She hung her head low and proceeded to explain. "Drew Moore was my husband. Cam murdered him over territory. When the Cubans found out Cam took over, he was left responsible for all of my husband's property—including me. At first it was real hard, but I learned to deal with it. He treated me okay until you came around."

"Well, who is Nancy Brown...I mean, Nancy Johnson? Y'all have me all confused."

"Why are you so damn inquisitive? Don't you know the less you know the better off you are! That's why I'm in this mess as it is."

"Just tell me!"

"Nancy Johnson is Cam's lieutenant's mother."

"His lieutenant...Prince?" I asked, with an are-you-sure facial expression.

"Yes, Prince...you heard me correctly."

"Oh, my God! So, Prince is Mya's father? I went and sat next to Nikki on the bed. I didn't care about the sex stains or Kenny being in the other room. That's why he came every week—to spend time with his daughter. "How did that happen? Well, I know how it happened, but why is Cam claiming Mya as his own?"

"Because Cam feels the need to control everything and everybody. Don't you get it by now, Mona? Drew and Prince were on top of the world. Cam was under the authority of Prince before he killed Drew. Since Cam took it upon himself to be the boss, that's exactly what happened—he became the boss. It's bigger than Cam, though. He's still suffering from the issues of losing control of his own family. That's why he's so demanding. He wants to make sure people in his circle are in line. Open your eyes! And don't for one minute get me wrong. I loved my husband dearly, but Prince was so compassionate and gentle. He showed me the utmost respect after my husband died. Before long we were sleeping together. He probably had the same effect on you." I didn't respond.

"Later, I found out I was pregnant. It couldn't have been my husband's because I was three months.

My husband died four months earlier. I was uncertain if it was Prince's because I was sleeping with Cam also. When I had Mya, I knew I couldn't tell Cam that she wasn't his. At the same time I didn't want to disrespect Prince by naming Cam as the father, so I left the father's name off of the birth record. Cam had a feeling Mya wasn't his. That's when he asked for a blood test. I refused, but he had it done anyway. He found out that Mya wasn't his around the time he met you. He never told anyone 'cause to him that would've ruined his image. Prince knows because I told him, but Cam doesn't think he knows. Granny is the only other person who knows the truth. Please keep this to yourself. You don't want to end up like me."

"So, that's why he's so angry with you. Does he have any idea that Prince is the father?"

"Yes, that's why he keeps him close. Cam is a beast, Mona. Save yourself some money to send to your family, 'cause he's not gon' let you go freely. At least leave them with some comfort. That's what I did for Mya. Miss Nancy gon' make sure she okay."

"What about Granny?"

"She won't get involved. She's a neutral source. I never understood that. That's one of the reasons I left, because she treated me...her own grandchild, like an outsider. She turned a blind eye to what Cam did to Drew and how he treats me."

The conversation was abruptly interrupted with a knock. "Peaches, you wanna hit this pipe?" Kiesha asked.

"Peaches?" I was baffled. "Hit the pipe...damn, Nikki, you are too good for this shit!" I may not have liked her much, but I did feel some concern.

"That's my name, now," Nikki responded. "Go ahead and get out of here, and   remember what I said. Be safe."

I put my head down so Nikki wouldn't see the worry on my face. I wanted to give her a friendly hug, but she turned her back to hit the glass pipe. I walked past the rooms in a hurry. By now Cam was looking for me. Instead of riding the elevator I took the steps, but neither exit was safe. I stepped over crackheads sprawled out on the stairwells. One of them grabbed my heel, causing me to slip. I got up and ran down the remainder of the steps as fast as I could. "Get away from me, you dirty bastard!" I screamed to the top of my lungs. "Leave me alone!"

Finally, I pushed the first floor stairwell door open and tried to pace myself. Where the hell was the Jeep? I knew somebody didn't steal it with Cam right on the spot. I looked around for Cam. He was nowhere in sight. Even the Hummer was gone. It was getting dark and the night-lights were coming on. *Oh shit, what am I going to do? Calm down, it's gon' be all right*, I told myself.

The sound of a stranger appeared from nowhere. "Honey dip, are you lost?"

"No, I'm not lost, but have you seen Cam?"

"Providing information will cost you," the man howled out before coming into full view. He was filthy, and I could tell that he was looking to get his next hit. I handed him twenty dollars. "Cam left from here twenty minutes ago, mad about some tape that nigga Controversy selling," he said, eyeing me from head to toe.

"V-i-d-e-o-t-a-p-e?" I said slowly. The man didn't respond. I handed him another twenty-dollar bill.

"Yeah, they said it featured his main girl getting freaked out." Apparently, he didn't know that I was the main girl.

"Thanks for the information," I replied.

"For another twenty, I'll tell you what the reward is for the person who finds her," he said persuasively.

"Okay, but I'll give you a hundred if you share that information and tell me the best way to get to East New York by foot."

"Sure will, hand me the money first!" I placed a crisp one-hundred-dollar bill in his hand. "That crazy fool put a fifty-thousand-dollar reward out for her safe return," he said, before giving me directions. "So, honey dip, if you come across her, she worth fifty thou'."

"Thanks again," I responded, before getting on my way. My head was hung so low that it almost touched my breast. I could feel the pulse of my feet each time they hit the concrete. It was cold outside and the wind blew across my face. At least it had stopped raining. My mind was racing. Controversy was a scandalous nigga. He promised me that he wouldn't show the tape. Wait a minute. Why should he have been true to me with all the things I'd done? I was a conniving, no good whore-ass groupie who would lie, cheat and steal to get what I wanted. I had the spirit of my mother before she found Christ. The sad part was that I wasn't even nineteen years old yet. I was a young woman trying to live beyond her years. But was that so bad? My mama taught me to take all that I could from a man. I was just following her instruction, right?

Chapter 16

The Chase

Escaping the area safely, I still had some unfinished business to tend to. Even though Cam had it in for me, I felt it necessary to talk with Prince. Inside I was truly sorry for treating him so badly. Besides, he was the only person who could talk sensibly to Cam. He was my only hope for a one-way ticket home without injury.

I approached the building feeling a little fearful, not knowing how Prince or Dawn would receive me. Forgetting what apartment they lived in, I came up on two little girls playing jacks in the hallway.

"Hi, girls. Do you live on this floor?"

"Yeah, why?" asked one of the little girls very forwardly. From the looks of it, her hair hadn't been combed for weeks. She had dried snot in the crevices of her nose. The clothing she wore was too small.

"I'm looking for Dawn," I responded. "Do you know which apartment she lives in?"

"Down there, on the right side of the tunnel," said the girl, pointing toward the end of the hall.

"Thank you, little girl." I handed her twenty dollars. She ran off, ecstatic about the money she'd just received.

Before I got a chance to knock on the apartment door Prince was coming out, and by the look on his face, he wasn't glad to see me. "What the hell are you doing here?" He grabbed me by my collar and pushed my body against the filthy cement wall. This was the first time I'd ever seen him this upset. "I told you, you aren't worth shit. Look what you've done to yourself now. Niggas all around Brooklyn projects, and probably in the Bronx projects by now, are watching your nasty ass on tape. Did you have to let him blindfold and handcuff you to the bed? Do you realize that not only him, but also ten other niggas had sex with you? Every time he left the room another dude came in."

Tears almost rolled down my face, but I desperately held them back. "Prince, I had no idea that I was with other guys. You have to believe me! Why doesn't anyone ever believe me?"

"Is your shit that ruined that you couldn't tell the difference in sizes? You still don't get it, do you?"

"No, I guess I don't get it. I'm tired of everybody telling me that! My eyes are wide open. I can see!"

"Yeah, I know, Mona, and the sad part is that your vision is very blurry." He looked at me in total disgust. "Didn't it dawn on you that all he wanted was to hit? He got what he wanted and others did too! He's going on about his life like you never existed. He doesn't care about your dumb ass! If you'd done your research, you may have familiarized yourself with his history of porn flicks for the public. Learn this lesson: life is not about letting this dude and that dude screw you for money. Maybe I'm giving you too much credit. I bet you did it for free. Imagine that—now the nigga is making money off pimpin' you! You are one stupid young girl. Status, money and power move you. You're ambitious for all the wrong reasons. All these things you can achieve by yourself. Instead you thrive off of men who screw you, mistreat you and assassinate your character—and all for what? You can't ever show your face around here anymore. You're labeled now—not as a hustler's wife, but as a trick bitch. And not for nothing, but, that's all you are, or, better yet, a groupie. You're washed up and labeled a dead woman in Cam's eyes. I can't help you with that, if that's what you came here for."

My manipulation game was out of the question. He was finished with me. "Prince, please!" I begged. "Just help me get to the train station"

"And jeopardize my life—for you—not for a kilo of coke! Your best bet is to hurry before Cam makes his rounds. I should call him right now, fifty thou' soundin' real good to my ears. To think, at one point I was contemplating taking you away from him—move to

North Carolina or something. What a laugh! A trick is never worth the trouble."

My feelings were deeply bruised. His words found their way straight to my heart. I decided to use my last bit of ammunition. "Cam will sure be pleased when he finds out that not only were you hitting me off, but you also fathered Mya," I said vindictively. I turned with a jerk and ran down the hallway.

"Don't worry," he replied, "by the time he finds out, I'll be long gone. You and Nikki are two of a kind!" What was I going to do? If Prince wouldn't help me, I knew nobody would.

After running for blocks I stopped to catch my breath. My heart was racing. The heels on both of my boots had broken off. I felt as though I was on a seesaw with each step I took.   People on the streets just watched me in my desperate state. It had been a long day. First my mom and now this.

How I wished I was back home watching the neighborhood from the stoop, or walking down the block, watching squatters going in and out of boarded-up houses. Right now, being a *blockhead* wasn't sounding too bad.

My legs began to feel heavy and I was ready to give up. Maybe Mommy wasn't crazy at all for giving her life to God. If he could turn her life around, I knew he could do something with mine.

Looking both ways to cross the intersection, I noticed a black Hummer, almost creeping down the street.

"Oh, shit, it's him, it's him!" I yelled. My legs wouldn't move fast enough, and before I knew it, Cam was looking directly at me. I stood in a trance like a stunned deer.

"Why?" he asked. "For the most part, I did right by you. You had to have him, didn't you? It was your way no matter what. You had to feed that desire to be with him. He's a bum. I told you that from the door. Now look how he put you out there. What, my love wasn't good enough that you had to be with several niggas to make up for it? I was looking forward to you having my first child—a beautiful little girl with your beautiful brown eyes." I looked around for a quick escape. "There's no need to look around. We've been watching you since you left Prince's house. Now, I know why you two were so close. He was hitting, too. Damn, you are a trick! I made the mistake of letting you stay at Granny's instead of sending you with Nikki. Because of your betrayal, you owe me your life."

Across the street a bus pulled up along the sidewalk. I saw this as my only escape. Using all of my energy, I ran across the street as fast as I could, just missing an oncoming vehicle. My heels ached with every step. I jumped on the bus and motioned for the driver to go. He looked at me like I was out of my mind. The people on the bus just stared. I ducked low, limping with every step, hoping to cause Cam to question whether I got on the bus or kept running through the neighborhood. "Driver, what is the destination of this bus?"

"Grand Central Station, young lady," he responded.

"Thank God!" I said with a sigh of relief.

When we arrived at the train station, I immediately checked for the next train leaving to Delaware. It was one o'clock in the morning and the next train was scheduled to leave at six o'clock. Five hours away...that was too much time! But what else was I going to do? I had no transportation. All I could do was pray and hope that six o'clock would arrive soon. I couldn't call home. They would be worried sick. I sat in the corner watching everyone that passed, scared to go to sleep. Maybe school wasn't that bad after all—the basketball games, skipping class and hanging out with my friends...those were the days. Most of my friends had gone to college to pursue a field of study. Instead of following them, I chose to pursue a career in chasing men. Inside I felt horrible, worthless, even. All those spirits of whoredom, thievery and cheating had finally caught up to me. I never wanted to be like my mother, but in essence, I was her all over again. Oh, what had I done to myself? The same demons that controlled her had now taken over me. Her seed, that bad seed, was sown into me. *Oh Lord! Please have mercy on my soul.*

To pass the time, I opened my bag and began writing in my journal. I wrote for hours, putting down on paper every event, occurrence and encounter of my life since graduation. I finished with a letter to my mother.

Dear Mom,

After all these years I am so happy that you gave your heart to the Lord. However, there are still some issues we need to deal with. You haven't been the best role model, but I love you nonetheless. For years I was angry with you. I couldn't wait until I turned eighteen. My teenage years were wicked. I loathed the fact that you chose men over me. What did I ever do to deserve that? For that matter, what did your son do? Never once did any of those men take him under their wing and show him how to be a man. Aren't you the least concerned about how he's turned out?

I'm angry, but the love I have for you overpowers that. You don't know how good I feel about the way you have changed. For once, people are coming up to me and are raving about how spiritual you are. How you like that? I love it dearly! I don't know, maybe this is Divine Intervention. It has to be, all the men and crack pipes you done been through...no disrespect; I'm keeping it real with you. If I never learned anything from you, I learned how to speak my mind. I know you think I'm headed in the same direction as you. But don't trip, my game is a little tighter than yours. Mom, I love you...I just had to say that before I continued on.

Don't worry yourself over my mistakes. Only God can correct them. All I ever wanted from you was unconditional love—the love I never received. It's okay, though. Right now, I'm almost at the point of positive change. Maybe we can start fresh and new. Around *town you may hear some bad things about me. Please don't think any less of me. Evil spirits can consume the best of us. Continue to pray for my well being until we reunite. This journal will account for my life since June of 2002. Maybe this will give you a better understanding of the seed you've sown. This way when I come home, we can battle these demons together. If by chance you don't see me in about five days after receiving this journal, open the first package. It contains over a million dollars. See to it that the church gets at least ten percent of it. Give another $50,000 to Nee for her daughter's education. Make sure Yatta gets $200,000 and tell him, get his! Start a foundation in my name to help "at risk" females in Delaware. Create a college trust fund for individuals in need. I also have plans on opening up a shoe store called "Precioustymes Feet Boutique." What do you think about that?*

Make sure you buy a nice home for you and Grandma. The rest of the money you can put aside for the necessities. Remember, that's only if I'm not home in five days; otherwise, leave my money alone. Love Ya! Till next time...Precioustymes, Mona

P.s. Cam should be the first suspect if something does happen to me! He's wicked. Don't believe nothing he tells you.

I pulled the last manila envelope, wrinkled and all, from my pocketbook. I placed the journal inside and put it in the nearest mailbox slot. At least I had money—the money I had stolen from Cam.

My father's people lived in North Carolina. I didn't need to go with Prince. When I arrived home, I would call him for the contacts and start my life over fresh and new—maybe give my heart to the Lord. This time I would do it right. My focus was going to be strictly on college.

All passengers leaving for Delaware please board now! Hearing that announcement warmed my soul. I felt at ease knowing the train had arrived.

Chapter 17

Going Home

The train ride allowed me to get some rest. I felt like I hadn't slept in days. Wiping the slobber from my mouth, I almost forgot my heels were off my boots. Damn! What were people going to think when I walked out of the train station? I gathered my Coach bag and walked through the station with pride as if I was still that chick. Realizing that I needed to use the bathroom, I made a pit stop. My stomach was bubbling. The bathroom was empty and boy was I glad of that. It seemed like I hadn't pooped in a week. I had to freshen up before I made my grand appearance anyway. The mall was my first stop. The store manager at one of the boutiques never had a problem with me using the dressing room to change. I'd done it a thousand times before.

I left the ladies room feeling like a new woman. Taking the first step out of the Wilmington station, I closed my eyes, breathed in deeply and exhaled. Finally, I had made it home. When I opened my eyes, I came face to face with death. It was Alexander King! My heart dropped. He stared at me with those once beautiful but now lifeless eyes. I tried to avoid making eye contact with him, but my pride wouldn't let me. I couldn't go out like that. I had made it this far, why should I turn back now? I didn't want him to win, at least not by cheating me out of my opportunity to change. But what was my fate? Was this the ultimate payback for all the times I mistreated people—for all the times I lied, cheated and deceived to advance? The distraught look on his face told me he had actually fallen in love with me. I decided that I'd use this to my advantage.

"What, you thought it was over?" The words he spoke grinded slowly between his clenched teeth. "I'm the man! Don't you ever forget that! I made you who you are today. If it weren't for my connections, you and your broke-ass family members would be starving right now. Look at you, you look disgusting!"

This was my last attempt to control the situation, and I had to use my best technique. "But wait, baby, we don't have to end it like this! I understand what you've been going through. I'm sure your mother is turning in her grave right now seeing your actions. She didn't want this for you and Kenny. You're so much better than that. All of the anger, the stress, the tension...I can help you. We can help each other overcome. Controversy set me up. And yes, I'm wrong for being so weak and so persistent in wanting him physically. I admit to that, but no one has ever made me feel the way you have. Many times at Granny's I cried myself to sleep worrying about you. Even when I didn't receive a courtesy call, I worried."

"There you go testing my intelligence again, Mona! Who do you think I am, a *Joe-Blow* sucka type? My lust for you grew until love consumed my heart, and you took that for granted. You toyed with my true feelings, and I can't let you live for that. My feelings are not to be taken lightly. I will always be the man! I told you before you will never be able to escape me. And like I tell all my victims, no one ever sees me coming. That's how I always catch my prey—with their eyes closed."

His words were slow and vicious. "But, please!" I begged.

"Shut up! No more words from those corroded lips! What man have they not been on—Controversy, Prince...did Kenny hit to?"

"No, I would never cross that line! Don't even play me like that, Camron. I may be frisky but I do have morals!"

"You are absolutely right—very loose morals! Goodnight, Mona Foster." Water filled the corners of his eyes. "I told you, I would never let anyone else hurt you beside me, and I'm here to put you out of your misery."

I was speechless. I felt blinded. There was nowhere to run. There wasn't anywhere to hide.

If only I knew skipping college would result to this.

If only I knew the spirit of my mother would dwell in me.

If only I knew how to deal with my issues.

If only I knew my eyes were blinded to sin.

If only I knew the Lord.

Lord, please save my soul.

Pushing me against a glass door, he pulled out a black Mac-10, pointed it to my head and pulled the trigger. The glass shattered as blood splattered against the walls. My head slammed against the door, and I felt my life begin to slip away. The huge hole sent blood spilling down my body. It was so much blood, too much blood that covered me. I saw daylight, and then I saw darkness. I could no longer hear the

people's screams. It became silent, and I became still.
No doubt it was over. I was going home.

**For I acknowledge my transgressions: and my
sin is ever before me.**
Psalm 51:3 - KJV

....

Miss Rhonda knelt down, deep in prayer. A
strong feeling of emptiness came upon her. She
screamed in agonizing pain. *Mona! Mona! Lord No!*

**The fathers shall not be put to death for the
children, neither shall the children be put to death
for the fathers: every man shall be put to death for
his own sin.**
Deuteronomy 24:16 – KJV

Chapter 18

The Service

The funeral was overcrowded. It was held in what seemed to be a tiny church. Eighth Street Baptist was capable of seating five thousand people. The turnout for Mona's funeral was all love, even with a closed casket. Over a hundred sprayed, cross-shaped, heart-shaped and star- shaped blue flowers with large gold bows streamed to the floor and flooded the temple. On top of the casket, in blue and gold fancy writing, the letters M-O-N-A were prominently displayed. The casket itself was sky blue, outlined with gold trimming. In Mona's memory, the church lowered the wide, seventy-inch movie screen.

Mourners watched as pictorial collages of her flashed across the screen. Her best friend, Nee, folded over in inconceivable pain every time she saw a different picture of them together.

Most of the hustlers from Fifth the forklift were present. Lil' Dee, Do Good, Blunt, Ali, Kevous, Dale, Bird and Maine represented lovely for Yatta, their gang leader. Yatta did his best to keep his composure while trying to hold his mother together. For a mother who had just lost a child, Miss Rhonda was doing her best. From time to time, a heartfelt scream would be heard, coming from the depths of her soul.

Yatta knew that Cam had a hand in his sister's murder. If he didn't, he would pay anyway. Only time would tell when. Yatta insisted that the Forklift wear black T-shirts in place of the white ones for her funeral and that previous boyfriends wear blue to represent the love they had for her. The Won Sumth'n Clique dressed in all white to celebrate Mona's victory in receiving her angel's wings. Each of the girls rolled up her left sleeve to expose the tattoo that linked them with their fallen leader. All the dudes in blue who fell victim to her were visibly shaken. Yatta was surprised by the damn near forty young men who showed up dressed in blue. He only knew of ten dudes that his sister had been with. If forty was the actual number, he had clearly underestimated her.

Cam boldly wore a dark red suit, advertising the blood shed by his hands. Richey, Earl and Slowdown accompanied him to the funeral, looking more than ready for a night at the club. Richey wore on an iced out Bezel watch with a bracelet to match. A big, ten-carat diamond hung from his left ear and a thirty-inch platinum chain with a heavy diamond cross hung from his neck. He stood about 6'4" and weighed 320 pounds easily. When he stepped into the room, everyone gasped as if they came face to face with Suge from *The Row*. Earl and Slowdown were older versions of basketball stars Vince Carter and the rapper Sticky Fingers from the group *Onyx*. They both had deep-set eyes, accented by silky black eyebrows. And perfect pearly white teeth that could have easily been mistaken as false, accented their wide smiles. However, in an instant, those beautiful smiles could be turned into something inhuman. Most people assumed that they were brothers because of all their similarities.

As soon as Nee spotted Cam she screamed, "It was him! It was him! He's the cause of Mona's death!" For a moment all eyes were on Cam, but when he sympathetically dropped his head, appearing to be grief stricken, they turned away.

The spiritual leaders called on God to restore the minds of the young individuals that were in attendance. Reverend Jones was the officiator of the service. As he began to speak, some people walked to the back, knowing that two weeks before the rev got busted with a semi-automatic pistol in his crib. Somebody was trying to rob him, but after hearing three shots, they decided against it. Rev was going to protect his, no matter who was on the receiving end!

"Please don't leave, you are about to hear a powerful word from God," Reverend Jones stated. "Let us bow our heads in prayer. Oh, most precious Father, Heavenly Father, the Alpha and Omega, the deliverer, the spiritual changer, we come to you now, Lord, asking you to forgive us of our sins. Asking you to deliver us from evil. Asking you to show mercy and grace upon us. This day, Lord, is bestowed to you. As we sit in the pews, open our minds, our hearts to what sayeth the Lord. Let us not take for granted the life you graciously let us live. Even if the conditions look grim, help us to see the brighter side, just as you have for our dearest sister, Mona Foster. Punish the man that did these awful things to her—the awful man who took her life when her young spirit desired to grow. Lord, she was just getting started as so many of the young people in this room today."

Slowdown eased from his seat and hollered, "Enough of this bullshit, we'll be here all night!" He didn't like the idea of making an appearance, let alone sitting through the whole ordeal.

Reverend Jones continued on. "Lord, forgive the sinner for he knows no better, and you said it in your word, Father, forgive them, for they know not what they do. Open up hearts to receive this word, in Jesus name we pray, Amen.

"We are gathered here today for the home going services for Miss Mona Foster, a beautiful and intelligent young lady whose life was ended trying to find her way back home. You ought to know one thing—we were all born to die. How you die is the one-million-dollar question. Do you think Mona wanted to die this way? If she were here today, what would she say? I'm imaging she'd say 'No.' I only met this young lady once or twice as a juvenile. She was one of the leaders of youth bible study; so I'm sure that in the midst of her situation she knew to call on God to deliver her from evil. Oh yes, oh yes, I truly believe that. Usher, fetch me some cold water, I'm fit'na preach in here today." He wiped his face with a white cotton towel as if he had worked up a real sweat. Before the glass of water arrived, ushers were tending to individuals as they worshipped and praised the spirit of God. "That's right, that's right, give praises to the Lord."

After about thirty-five minutes of continuous preaching and praise, Reverend Jones began his closing. "Young people, young people, I say take heed to the message Mona is trying to give you. It's time to stop running away from God and start running toward the kingdom of heaven." Many spiritual leaders shouted, giving glory to God. A few began to speak in tongue.

"Know that you are a temple of God. Use your God conscience to make good judgment and better decisions for your life. Those of you who have not entered into a relationship with God can do so by coming to the altar today. I know it's crowded with all the beautiful blue and gold flowers, but find a space somewhere so we can pray with you."

At least a hundred souls got saved on the strength of paying respect to the Won Sumth'n leader, Mona Foster. Even though she was a dirty playa in the game, God used her to deliver others.

When Cam eased his way to the front, Nee screamed out, "Look at the devil. You need to stop playing with the Lord, you murderer." He continued on as if he couldn't comprehend the words that boldly escaped from her mouth.

To lighten the mood of the service, one last picture of Mona, mooning her high school graduation class, was shown. To end the ceremony, the choir sang their version of *How Do I Say Goodbye to Yesterday?* Yatta, Do Good, Kevous, Cam, Richey, Earl and Slowdown slowly lifted the casket down the aisle as weeping could be heard both loudly and silently. Mona was   another young soul being put to rest from a violent crime.

Righteousness exalteth a nation: but sin is a reproach to any people.

Proverbs 14:34

Epilogue

I pray that you understood the message behind *Blinded.* Every day we encounter individuals like Mona Foster. Maybe at some point in your life, if not currently, you knew an individual like Mona Foster. Maybe you *are* Mona Foster.

This urban tale, by no means, was an effort to portray the negativity of street life. It was written to give you the opportunity to look within and examine any foul thoughts, behaviors and actions of not only yourself, but family and friends as well. I pray that you are the praying warrior, fighting for all the lost souls, because I am.

Many people believe in the African proverb that says, "It takes a village to raise a child." See, what they don't realize is that the village *is* raising their child/children! The hustler on the corner, the drug addicts, the number runners, the armed robbers, the murderers, the unfaithful wife and husband, the young lady chasing the hustler and the list goes on. This is the so-called *village* that is raising the child.

The village is nothing more than the community. I'm not just talking about urban neighborhoods, but suburban neighborhoods as well. Trust me, they encounter the same issues, only theirs is concealed behind closed doors.

We still want to believe that Big Mama, a.k.a. Grandmom, will always be there to help us out—get us out of the situation. We need to get that out of our minds! We all very well know that Big Mama is the missing link! But she no longer resides in the home or in the community. We've put her in a nursing home, or by the grace of God, she has been laid to rest. She was the one holding the family together. Now it's time for us to take a stand.

If you're a parent, it is your responsibility to step it up, or you may be faced with a Mona Foster. *You* must be the role model for your children—not the athletes, musicians and actors. Your children are the image of you, whether good or bad. Until you open your eyes and grasp the concept of *Sowing Positive Seeds,* you will continue to fail as a parent.

The sad part is that most of us don't even acknowledge our attitudes of indifference. We stay stuck in our *Stinking Thinking* mode. It won't be until we acknowledge and open our eyes to positive change, that change occurs. We must tackle negative spirits with the power of God.

Mona's mother tried to intercept, but only after Divine Intervention. That was a blessing, but her timing was way off. By the time she realized that Mona was in trouble, she knew her daughter was dwelling deep in sin. Mona recognized that she had issues but did not accept full responsibility, thinking she had a long life ahead of her.

I hate to be the bearer of bad news, but time waits for no man. Granted, not everyone is open for Divine Intervention. That's why God allows tragedies such as incarceration, paralysis, life-threatening disease, disability, mental destruction, severe depression or the death of a loved one to change us. This is when we reach our breaking point. During these times we are humble. This humility either creates positive change or causes us to dwell deeper in our sins. Hopefully, it's not too late for any of us. I pray that we all have accepted and acknowledged our negative behaviors.

If you have not already done so, assume your position! Make a positive change to empower and encourage those that follow in your footsteps! Don't wait until it's too late. Do it now!

Father, I thank you for the reader. I thank you for how you have changed my life. I thank you for how you delivered me. I thank you for dwelling in my midst. I pray that everyone who reads, or even touches or skims through this book becomes so richly blessed in spirit. In all that I/we do, allow it to be for your glory. Allow us to absorb your spirit. Show us our purpose in this life and how to use our purpose for your glory. Make positive changes in our lives where we need it most. Enter into our mind, soul and spirit. Lord, we give you continuous thanks and praise. In Jesus name we pray. Amen.

May God continue to bless you! Thank you for your support.

One Love, One Spirit!

Till next time...Precioustymes!

KaShamba

Check out other titles on:

www.triplecrownpublications.com

www.precioustymesentertainment.com

You may email me at:

Precioustymesent@aol.com

ORDER FORM

Triple Crown Publications
2959 Stelzer Rd.
Columbus, Oh 43219

Name: _____

Address: _____

City/State: _____

Zip: _____

		TITLES	PRICES
		Dime Piece	$15.00
		Gangsta	$15.00
		Let That Be The Reason	$15.00
		A Hustler's Wife	$15.00
		The Game	$15.00
		Black	$15.00
		Dollar Bill	$15.00
		A Project Chick	$15.00
		Road Dawgz	$15.00
		Blinded	$15.00
		Diva	$15.00
		Sheisty	$15.00
		Grimey	$15.00
		Me & My Boyfriend	$15.00
		Larceny	$15.00
		Rage Times Fury	$15.00
		A Hood Legend	$15.00
		Flipside of The Game	$15.00
		Menage's Way	$15.00

SHIPPING/HANDLING (Via U.S. Media Mail)   **$3.95**

TOTAL $_____

FORMS OF ACCEPTED PAYMENTS:

Postage Stamps, Institutional Checks & Money Orders, all mail in orders take 5-7 Business days to be delivered.

ORDER FORM

Triple Crown Publications
2959 Stelzer Rd.
Columbus, Oh 43219

Name: _____

Address: _____

City/State: _____

Zip: _____

		TITLES	PRICES
		Still Sheisty	$15.00
		Chyna Black	$15.00
		Game Over	$15.00
		Cash Money	$15.00
		Crack Head	$15.00

SHIPPING/HANDLING (Via U.S. Media Mail)   **$3.95**

TOTAL $_____

FORMS OF ACCEPTED PAYMENTS:

Postage Stamps, Institutional Checks & Money Orders, all mail in orders take 5-7
Business days to be delivered.

"MENAGE A' TROIS Sexy Flicks"
The Ultimate in Visual Entertainment

Experience visual entertainment at its best! Our photos of sexy ladies will take you far and beyond your imagination.

Order a Sampler Set today for only $9.99* + Shipping & handling $2.00 (Assortment of (10) Hot photos)
Send $2.00 for a preview Color Catalog+$2.00 shipping & handling
Send $6.00 for a multi-page Color Catalog-Includes Free shipping

Quantity	Item	Price
	"Sampler Set" (Assortment of (10) Hot photos)	$9.99
	Preview Catalog	$2.00
	Full Catalog **(INCLUDES FREE SHIPPING)**	$6.00
	Merchandise Total	
	Shipping & Handling	$2.00
	Total	

Send All Payments To:
MENAGE A' TROIS
2959 Stelzer Road Suite C
Columbus, OH 43219

*The Sampler Set is pre-selected
 This is a limited time offer.

(As of January 2005)
*Free shipping & handling applies to full catalog orders only.